OUT OF THE DARKNESS

OUT OF THE DARKNESS

RICH LAMONICA

The MisFitNation LLC

CONTENTS

Out of The Darkness
By
Rich LaMonica

Dedication

This Book is dedicated to all those who raised their right hand and put themselves in harm's way.

Forward

Indeed, every decision we make in life carries consequences, and this is particularly true for those who choose to serve in the military, especially in countries with global responsibilities and potential risks. The decision to join the military is a profound one, as it involves not only dedicating oneself to a career but also committing to a higher calling of service and sacrifice.

For young men and women who decide to enlist, it often starts as a personal journey of self-discovery and purpose. They may be drawn to the military for various reasons, such as a desire to make a difference, a sense of duty to their country, or a longing for camaraderie and belonging.

Once they don the uniform, they become part of a tradition that extends back through history, where they inherit the collective experiences and legacies of those who came before them. As world leaders, their country's military personnel must be prepared to defend and protect the values and principles their nation stands for, which can mean facing dangerous and complex challenges.

Every deployment or mission carries with it a unique set of risks and uncertainties. The decisions made by these young men and women can have far-reaching consequences not only for their own lives but also for the lives of others and the overall geopolitical landscape. The responsibility they bear is immense, and they must constantly be ready to adapt and react to rapidly changing situations.

Throughout their service, they encounter numerous decisions that test their courage, resilience, and ethical judgment. The choices they make in moments of adversity can have profound effects on the safety and well-being of their comrades, the civilians they protect, and the success of their missions.

While some decisions may bring success and fulfillment, others might lead to heartache, trauma, and emotional burdens that stay with them long after their service ends. Each day in the military is a series of decisions, from following orders on the battlefield to supporting their fellow service members in times of need.

Despite the challenges and sacrifices, these young men and women find purpose and pride in their service. They recognize that their choices contribute to a broader mission of safeguarding their nation and upholding the values they hold dear. In making the decision to join the military, they embrace a life of service that requires courage, commitment, and selflessness. They face the unknown with determination, knowing that their actions can impact the lives of countless others.

Ultimately, the decisions made by these young men and women in the military are a testament to their dedication to their country and their willingness to shoulder the responsibility of defending and safeguarding the world's freedom and security.

CHAPTER 1

Bull

There was a calming wind hitting Bull in the face. He was exhausted and lost in thought. Time is constant, and Bull knows this. One day his time just stopped, and he sat there with his head in his hands trying to figure out where it had gone. The last 14 years of his life had been a blur. What has become of him? Where were all of his friends? Time does not stop for anyone. His mind was filled with questions about what he has been through, what he has lost, and where he will possibly end up.

His pants were drenched in sweat and mud, he was leaning against a wall with his trusty M4 strapped against his chest and dangling. The smell of war was all around him, and he could care less. He worried about his team, were they whole? This was a repeat of many different occasions, not a bad replay but a replay at that. He knew this was his last dance with the devil and was taking it in. This was not supposed to end like this, and it was bothering him more than he thought it would.

How many times have they been on top of the mountain and working the problem? This scenario was running through his brain like a hamster on a wheel. This team he is on has changed many times over the years. People come and go due to orders and injuries or being taken from the earth. His head was pounding after being in the fight all day and knowing the cost that has been paid by many of his sisters and Brothers.

He made many friends along the way and led future leaders on this journey. He was always an outsider sitting on the inside, He was truly an Outcast a MisFit. There was not a mission he could not take on without being successful, and all knew this. His mind drifted to a way different time. He was a young punk on the streets of the city.

He used to have patience and was caring for others. His life now is in the now, it has to be immediate, or it does not happen. He cares for those who are in his circle but not any beyond that.

He did not have a ton of stuff growing up. He also never wanted for anything. He was the youngest of four in a hard-working lower-middle-class family. They had food, clothes, and family. Like most boys growing up, he stayed outside all day. When the lights came on the streets emptied of kids and became a different place.

The circle he was in as a kid was tight-knit and would do anything for each other. They played games in the streets. Traditional ones like football, stickball, and wiffleball. This list, of course, included manhunt (This would provide useful training for his future) and tag. There were games that were passed on to them from the older kids like scalsies.

Scalsies was a game that could take hours to play. First,

you had to get chalk and draw out the board. Starting in the lower right corner the number 1 is placed in a box, 2 in the upper left corner, 3 in the upper right, 4 in the lower left, 5 in the top left center, 6 lower right center, 7 left side center, 8 right side center and 9 in the bottom center-left and 10 in top center-right with the winning shot coming when you hit 11 in the center of the board. The players usually 4-6 kids would have bottle caps filled with melted crayons, it started with metal caps then with the introduction of the plastic milk jug all things went to plastic tops. The players would smooth out the bottom of them so they would slide better. After determining the order of play they would start from a start line and flick the caps towards the number 1 and if they landed in, they go again launching for 2 and so on. If they did not make it, they had to wait till their turn again. First, one to get through to the last number would win.

They had imaginations that would be exercised daily and usually ended up with them going home with scrapes, bruises, and the occasional broken bone. Kids were free to be happy and live a fun life.

Bull like all kids growing up would have friends that as they got to high school and beyond would drift very far apart. There was always a core group that stayed in touch and would go out of their way to do things with each other when in the same area.

Most of the group stayed in their hometown or within a 15-mile radius of it. 2 would leave and become leaders in the Military. Bull and Troy were in the Army and Air Force respectively. Each entered with different paths. One would be an officer and the other Enlisted. One earned his degree while becoming an officer, that is Troy. Bull started his degree pursuit after high school in accounting, then on to management, he even played two seasons of College Football before making the leap into the Army to get a fresh start. Their careers went on parallel to each other with both being successful at their craft....

CHAPTER 2

On Top of The Mountain

The smoke still laid heavy on the mountain top, the smell of spent munitions and blood was thick in the air. Afghanistan, if not for war, would be a beautiful country is all he could think at the moment.

16 hours earlier his team climbed to fight on this mountain. They were met by stiff and trained resistance for much of the climb. 2 hours into the climb, at the first plateau Tex, who was from Hawaii was shot through the left side of his vest and out the right. A big guy who could have been a defensive end in the NFL if he didn't choose to serve his country first, dropped like a sack of potatoes, with little to no noise besides the thud of him hitting the rocks beneath him. He was immediately in shock, as were most of the team. Doc jumped up and got to his side to start treating. Doc spoke calmly to Tex telling him he will be ok. He pressed his radio and asked for immediate medevac. Doc was our team medic; he grew up

on the streets of Compton and Long Beach. At the age of 8, he became the man of the house after his dad was killed in a drive-by shooting. His dad was his hero, a firefighter in Los Angeles and an Army Veteran. He got out of the city at the age of 18 went into the Army and was in the 75th Ranger Regiment during Desert Storm and Somalia. His dad taught him values every day and doc emulated him. The day he was killed it was mistaken identity, leaving Doc to take care of his two little sisters and help Mom. He followed his dad's footsteps and left for Fort Benning two days after graduating High School. He joined under a new directive to become a special forces soldier directly. He excelled and earned his Green Beret and Long Tab in the shortest time possible. He went on to the medic course and then joined our team in 2014.

With one teammate down and the rest fighting, Bull knew it was going to be a long day. Hollywood, his team leader was calling for close air support and directing us in the battle. He was called Hollywood because he always looked like he came out of make-up to star in a movie. His hair was always perfect. He grew up in rural Georgia, was a star athlete at his small county high school. He could run like the wind, and he was also strong as hell. When he got to the academy he stood out amongst his peers, he was 6'7 240 pounds of solid muscle and took charge immediately. Between his freshman and sophomore years, he attended Airborne and Air Assault Schools, the next year he went to pathfinder and before his senior year he crushed ranger school. He looked like a clothing sales hero as he arrived at Infantry officer basic course at Benning. He once again rose to the top and was sent to the 75th Ranger regiment. He stayed at Hunter Army Airfield and completed his Platoon Leader time going on two deployments and then went to SFAS and arrived at our team in 2014 a month after Doc. He and Tex were in the same selection course and were pretty tight.

Hollywood ran across the incoming fire to check on his friend and Doc. Doc told him it was severe and needed to get him out. Hollywood called me and Justice over. We dodged the bullets, and he asked if we would be willing to carry Tex down to a clear LZ and get him out. That was a no thought question, of course, we would, we do not leave our brothers. We picked him up, divvied up his ammo and gear then started our descent. We made it down to the clearing in 40 minutes. We could still hear heavy fighting above us. The only bird that would come close to the fight was from TF Pedro, the Airforce Pararescue dudes. They took Tex gave us two bags, 1 with ammo and 1 with medical supplies to climb up with. We had not heard much about the fight since we left, the team radioed ahead and asked for the bags and a QRF. The climb was deliberate now. We knew our guys were in a pinch if they requested this. There were only 6 of them up there fighting so they were trying to maneuver as fast as possible back to them. (3 core teammates stayed back at the Team house to maintain comms and launch support, if necessary, along with enablers). They also dropped off four enablers who could fit on the bird with the supplies.

Now 4 hours in we finally got comms back up with them and the chatter was not good. Hollywood was calling for close air support and continuously asking where the QRF was. Justice got on the mic and asked the vicinity location and plotted a course for us to enter from the east. We got

Hollywood on our internal line and asked for a sitrep. He said he had 4 wounded including him, running low on Ammo, and nearly surrounded. When asked if they could still fight, he said fuck yes.

Justice got the course plotted and we started hauling ass up to them. We were now 400 meters from them and 6 hours into the climb. We could not see them, but we could hear the distinctive sounds of AK-47 and DShK (The DShK is a belt-fed machine gun that uses a butterfly trigger. Firing the 12.7×108mm cartridge at 600 rounds per minute) being shot at them. Justice again called up to ask for a grid. This time Doc got on and gave the correct grid and their heading. We were directly in front of them but had the enemy between us.

Justice was from a farming family in Idaho. He played college football at Iowa and then went to law school, he graduated, passed the bar, and decided he needed to serve his country first, so he enlisted in 2008 as an engineer. He went to Fort Leonard Wood for his basic and advanced individual training before heading to the 101st Airborne and A co 2 BSTB. He was a fast learner and went to sapper school as a Specialist and passed without any issues, his command rewarded him with a slot to ranger school three weeks later, he was tired but smoked it. In 2010 he went to SFAS and joined the team in 2012. He got the name Justice because of his law degree, and how he handed out pain to the enemy.

Justice had two long strands of C4 tied together with a length of det cord. He said he had an idea. I trusted his judgment and listened. He wanted to sneak around to the north of the enemy. Attach the strands through the trees there then maneuver back to just east of them. It would be at this time he would blow it and get their attention focused away. We could then push through and remove the rest of the threat. We radioed forward and told them they would have to lift and shift to make this work. We called on a direct link to Hollywood and he was very winded and talking low. We knew we did not have a lot of time.

It had been over 8 hours now since Tex was hit and 10 since we started this mission. Justice got the C4 placed, and we maneuvered to our next position. As the blast went off, we started rushing and blasting through the enemy stronghold. It became a slugfest, but we took out a good bit of their advantage with the blast. We each took two enablers and were able to get to the rest of the team. Doc was one of the two not wounded and took the bag of medical supplies immediately to help the others. He already verbally triaged them and went one by one to treat them while we all fought. I distributed the bag of ammo amongst everyone and made sure they were good. Hollywood was gray in his face and was still conducting the fight. Doc pulled him back to treat him and I was able to assume those duties. I got on with higher and asked about the status of QRF.

The QRF would not be able to get to our position for at least another 90 minutes after maintenance issues on the bird. A ground assault force of 12 moved out but the trek would take them even longer. The training allowed the team to work the problem throughout all this chaos for 11 hours now. Every member of this team had a solid case of resilience and calmness. It was showing now, in this time, just how resilient they were.

CHAPTER 3

Train-Up

Six months ago, the 12-man team went into the mountains of Colorado and stayed up there with just one bag each for two weeks. For those 14 days, each man had a task to track and provide meals for the rest of the team at least once. The day of your track was followed by a day of leading the Team on maneuvers through the mountains. It was not strange on this team to train the next man up, what was strange was that they chose to do it in extreme conditions. After those two weeks, they were flown back to team headquarters where they were each handed another bag and got on a Chinook provided by 160th Special Operations Aviation Regiment (SOAR). This was yet another difference on this team, when others would have gone to the Team Room, cracked a bottle, and called it an exercise, they were now wheels up. On the flight, Tex was joking as usual, and Doc was egging him on. Justice was trying to rest and leaning against Bourne. Bourne is the team intelligence chief and they named him after Jason Bourne. He grew up in Ponce, Puerto Rico, and was the youngest of 5 children. He joined the National Guard in PR when he was a Junior in High School. He became an Intelligence Analyst for the guard. He would take his job very serious and read up on every facet of war he could to become the best. He switched to Active Duty as a Sergeant and met an Intel Warrant who told him he needed to move over. He chased his next goal and crushed it. He was stationed with Doc with the Rangers and followed him to selection. They arrived at the team two months apart.

When the pilot got on the internal microphone, he gave the two minutes signal for all to get ready. Then one minute came then the back ramp dropped, and they started jumping out into the darkness and a body of water. All Bull could think was challenge accepted, pushed Switch awake, and said let's go. Switch was the team senior comms expert. He came from a mountainous region of North Carolina close to Boone. As a child, his father would take him into the trails and teach him survival techniques and tested him constantly. His father had served in Vietnam with the 173rd and did not want his son to be underprepared for anything. When he turned 18, they had a sit-down and spoke about the next steps. Switch decided the Army was his next obvious path. His dad drove him to Charlotte, and he signed up for Infantry with Airborne and Ranger in his contract. Growing up the way he did he was not the most social, but he was ruthless. He could shoot, move, and communicate better than most. He excelled through training and found himself with the 75th Rangers at Fort Benning. After 4 years there he too went to selection and joined the team as a communications Sergeant in 2015.

The helocast was fun, figuring out where the team actually was and navigating to a reference point for extraction was challenging. It was a three-day trek through marsh and swamps to get to an opening where they could rig a radio and call for extraction. When the bird landed at their base, they were picked up and taken to a hanger. In here the Group Commander and leadership team were present. This is where they were given the current mission. To hunt down and destroy splinter cells in the mountains of northeastern Afghanistan and in the tribal areas of Pakistan.

The next 5 months were loaded with language and traditional skill training to enhance their capabilities, it was also a whirlwind. The BBQ before deployment was the first time, they felt like they stopped in 6 months. It was much needed, and it lasted an entire weekend. Monday, they rolled into the Team room loaded up all gear and began the wait for the flight. Friday the C-17 arrived, and they loaded up. Sixteen hours later they were scheduled to arrive at FOB Fenty in Jalalabad, Afghanistan.

CHAPTER 4

Good-Bye

Any team that trains to go fight their nation's battles understands the sacrifice they are making. It is their loved ones who do not always have the same understanding. As they train up and become closer to each other, they are unfortunately straining an already fragile relationship at home.

Bull had been married for six years at the time train up started and was home maybe a third of it. During one of his home periods, his wife Hanna and him had their first and only child. They have gotten into a routine of not being too connected during these periods. Hanna and Shelly, now 4, were used to living their life while Bull lived his.

The reality of being in the military and having a family is that you will live two distinct lives for a majority of it. When Bull returned from the train-up he was focused on preparing his gear for the trip across the pond. Hanna was focused on keeping Shelly busy so she would not miss dad too much.

This time though, Bull was feeling off. He realized that

his marriage to Hanna and his relationship with Shelly was splintered and he wanted to repair it. On their two-week break from training and lift off, he planned a getaway in the mountains of North Carolina. He did it for two reasons, the first was to maintain his altitude training, and two for them to be off the grid the entire time.

This sort of helped the girls but made Bull realize what he had been doing the entire time. He knew he was mission-focused 100% of the time and family came only after all training was complete. He now understood the harm he was doing to his family and that started to mess with his head. He started to not feel invincible and worried about the girls if something would happen to him. He had seen a few friends get taken and the struggles that followed for them. He was convinced he was going to have everything ready for them if he is taken.

The goodbye was not easy for the small family unit. Hanna had been reading about the zone he was heading to and learning about how intense it was. She knew his heart was huge and would throw himself on a grenade for the sake of his teammates. That thought went through her mind constantly. They came back down the mountain and returned to base. She detached herself from him and allowed time for him to get his game face on.

This routine was not just in Bull's house but all the team that had family went through some sort of ritual before departing to fight. Some of the guys would send their families for spa days or get gifts for the kids that they had been asking for. Some of the spouses would retreat to routines that make them feel safe. This includes cleaning everything in the house over and over while ignoring all other things going on.

This is a weird set of rituals that go on in military families in all branches. The hardships attached are understood yet are not truly faced head-on by the families till they are back together again, many months later if ever. Many families made the reunion like a holiday. Drinks, food, and festivities were everywhere. Hanna had a ritual she would always do when Bull returned. She would arrive at the reunion site on base with a cooler full of beer and some snacks for the team. Then as he was in the shower at home she would make him his favorite meal, hotdogs, he truly was a simple man outside of the uniform.

CHAPTER 5

Crossing the Pond

The flight from the base in the states to Afghanistan takes Soldiers on a journey. They must go from point A in the states to an entry point in Germany where if lucky they are only there for a short period of time. This depends on the type of aircraft. In this case, the team was flying with the Air Force on a C-17. The plus of flying on this platform was you take all your gear with you, and you spread out on a seating pallet for the flight.

The negative is that nearly every Air Force flight across the pond winds up having "issues" when they land in Germany or Spain. These issues miraculously take enough time for the crew to check out local areas, reset and then get back in the air for the flight to their destination.

During this "layover", most teams would just relax and eat. This team decided to go for a five-mile run then go through tactics in the hangar all day. This is another thing that set this group of warriors apart from others, rest was not in their dictionary. They felt being "Switched On" was the best way to find success on the battlefield.

After a day plus of letting the Air Crew "fix" their craft. Hollywood called the team into a huddle. They would be departing in two hours. They would now stop in Kyrgyzstan to pick up a couple of enablers that were already waiting there. This stop would add another full day to the journey as the flight crew would now need their mandatory rest period after flying into the country.

The flight there was five hours most just relaxed or read up on culture in the area they were going to be operating. Once they landed Hollywood and Bull were given a brief by the liaison on the ground. This included where they could bunk for the night, what was available on the base to do, and of course where their enablers were located.

Bourne was sent to link up with the enablers and bring their senior people to meet with the team. These enablers included a Female Engagement Team (FET) a Joint Tactical Air Control (JTAC) team and a platoon of security force Soldiers to act as vehicle drivers and gunners as needed. Since they would have a full 24 hours in Kyrgyzstan, the team decided that was a good time to meld together with all the new pieces and get this relationship started the right way. Hollywood told the leaders to bring the rest of their people with them in 30 minutes and they would meet in front of the gym. He told them to be ready to put in three hours of work.

In the 30 minutes leading up to the big meet, Doc and Tex met with the dining facility manager and asked where they can source some steaks and all the fixings along with beers so this big new unit could have a BBQ and mesh together. Doc and Tex got a point of contact and met with the local man outside the base. They paid him and told him he had three hours and 15 minutes to have it ready. They had their liaison control his access and set him up near where they would stay the night.

With the planning complete they ran over to the gym to meet up with the team and all the enablers. It was now two in the afternoon local time. The security Soldiers were all young and wide-eyed as they saw the team for the first time. Bourne told them to lay their weapons on the table in front of him and then go get briefed by Hollywood. He then had a member of the liaison office pull security on them.

Hollywood was not a hype man; he was not a look at me dude. He was just a guy who liked the camaraderie and liked to use fitness and food to develop it. He welcomed the new teammates and had everyone introduce themselves, well not in the normal manner. The team now had over thirty members. They would each introduce themselves while on a run. Each member would have 2 minutes to tell the group about themselves and then call some cadence and then pass it back to the next person. In simple math, this equated to an hour just in introductions then cadence you could add another 45 minutes. That is right Hollywood took the entire new team on approximately a half-marathon welcome run. They all introduced themselves and were pumped the whole way.

When the run was finished a few of the security Soldiers were puking off to the side and one of the JTACs lay on the floor for a bit. The FET members were all fine and asked what was next. Bull was up next and had everyone get in a circle. He handed the person in front of him a 15 lb. medicine ball and told them to pass to their right. While the ball was passing around, he had everyone doing air squats. The ball made it around once, so they went to lunges, a second lap complete ass-kickers were introduced. When the Third Lap was complete, he led them to the row of pull-up bars where each member had to complete 10. While one was on the bar, one was spotting them and everyone else was doing pushups.

When the last group got on the bar and did their 10 a bell miraculously rang. Everyone was near empty on energy, but no one wanted to blink first. It was an awesome bonding workout. Tex got in front of everyone and gave them their next orders. He told them to meet outside the bunkhouse in 5 minutes. Many looked at him and said what is the bunkhouse. He was so used to speaking to his internal team he used their lingo. So, he explained to them where to go.

Five minutes later the entire team was in front of a feast. Hollywood welcomed them all to the Team. This was the team's new name as Hollywood was briefed earlier in the day. He told them to eat, drink and enjoy for in 12 hours we will be flying into the belly of the beast. We will hunt down and kill our enemies while protecting those who cannot protect themselves. He gave an amazing speech that in all the years of service Bull had could not be matched.

Everyone had a great time and got to know each other as best they could in a short period. This would be the start of a great team, a great work environment. The next day they all helped each other to load the C-17 with all the additional gear and passengers and took off for what will be Afghanistan.

CHAPTER 6

Afghanistan

Known as the graveyard of empires, this country has a long history of warriors. It has handled the British, Russians, and all others that have tried to enter and take over their country. Now in a long war with Americans in the country, it was looking like a no-win situation. The core team had read books on the country and the forces they would be in contact with. The Taliban was a huge study point for them along with the Haqqani network in their region.

They arrived in Bagram for an equipment draw. The C-17 refueled as soon as it finished its landing sequence. Half of the team took off in a bus to pick up gear identified by headquarters as being needed for the mission set. After an hour on the ground, the bus along with three trucks arrived at the aircraft. They unloaded all the gear and palletized it for shipment on the C-17 and the ride to their last fight stop in Jalalabad. The FET also got off and went to a headquarters on the sprawling airbase. They received some equipment and funds to further help them complete their internal missions in the region.

The flight to Jalalabad was relatively fast. As soon as they hit cruising altitude they dove in and swooped in for a landing to ensure they would not be targeted by any anti-aircraft capabilities the Taliban was in possession of. This marked the second time security Soldiers were puking. Most of them just laughed at them as they rolled to a stop on the far side of FOB Fenty. They would stay on Fenty for two days to ensure weapons still were top-notch and also to load their vehicles for the ride into Chowkay.

All the vehicles were loaded with gear and people, it was packed for their ride to their home for the next six months on Combat Outpost (CoP) Red Wine. They pulled in and met with the outgoing team 259. The next hours were spent getting people in hooches and getting an intelligence dump from 259. The information they shared was valuable to the planning of the first missions. They had been in the country for six months and were only in one firefight with the Taliban. The severity of which was intense, and they lost two vehicles. The premise of this fight was not a raid or a hit on a high-value target (HVT), it was a chance meeting between forces at an intersection when one decided to fight. The other relevance of this fight was it happened less than four days ago, so during the team's travel.

This was information that could have helped them in planning on their final two days of the journey however, it could not stop their movement. Hollywood wanted to sit with the outgoing team leadership and ask a bunch of questions in reference to this contact with the Taliban. The leadership of 259 seemed to not want to share all the details of how it happened with them. It was like they were covering something up. Or they were afraid to admit they made a very bad error.

Hollywood was at a loss for he knew the team leader from when they went to West Point together. He knew he was very strategic and planned everything down to the last detail. What could have caused this to happen?

The team did not care either way. On their train-up, they were planning on high-intensity combat and violent encounters with a determined enemy. This incident only showed them they trained hard for a valuable reason.

Day two in-country wound up being a ride along with the outgoing team. They pointed out areas of concern and made introductions to local leaders. In the afternoon there was a meal with the rest of the local leadership to introduce the new team. Most times these deals take a week to accomplish a good hand-off. In this case, 568 was not happy with 259 and sent them on their way. They had to deal with an investigation into the loss of the two vehicles and associated equipment and the injuries sustained by their security element.

CHAPTER 7

Mission Sets

The first week, the team split into four distinct groups. Each group was comprised of three operators a FET member, three security Soldiers, and a JTAC member. The groups went to all the villages within a five-kilometer circle of Red Wine. Each day was like Groundhog Day, the four elements would roll out in staggered formation. Every couple of hours a team would leave. By the time the last team was leaving the first that left was coming back in. The team that Bull was on was responsible for the south of the CoP. They went out each day and gathered valuable intelligence. The FET leader Lioness 7 was on this team. She was very good at intelligence gathering and making those who were difficult, feel comfortable talking.

The team called her Cali since she was from California. She was strong physically and mentally. She had a degree in social science and was extremely good at her job. On the last day of the week, she broke a local leader. He told her that the attack on the previous team occurred due to their lack of respect for the community. This led to the residents telling the Taliban all the routes that 259 used, along with types of vehicles and weapons.

Although the previous team only had one reported contact with the Taliban, they were heavy with their hands on the population. This led to the destruction of the two vehicles and the wounding of the security Soldiers. Two of them were still in hospitals having surgery to stabilize them for flights to Germany.

The elders provided pictures of the vehicles on previous missions. With targets drawn on some of team 259s members. The Taliban paid top dollar for this information and did not have to search to find people with it.

Cali did not make any promises, nor did she break any rules while extracting the information. She was just very persuasive in her tactics. This got Bull's attention along with Bourne. They knew they had a valuable asset in Cali and would leverage here talents for the rest of the tour.

Cali was born and raised in San Diego. Her dad was a Seal in the 80s and into Desert Storm. He retired not long after that and settled outside Coronado so he could be a civilian instructor for BUDS. Cali idolized him and would beg him to take her to training events all the time. She could not wait to join the military and she did so right out of High School. She knew she could not go into Special Operations like her dad due to regulations and restrictions on women, so she asked for Airborne and Human Intelligence for the time being.

She excelled as a Human Intelligence (HUMINT) Soldier and kept up her physical training to maintain optimal fitness.

Her education in intelligence only enhanced how good she could become. On her first deployment she was assigned to a Brigade Combat Team out of Fort Bragg. She was in a HUMINT platoon. They were operating in southern Afghanistan and the fight was kinetic daily. Cali never flinched while on mission and proved herself as an asset.

Each day after all missions were complete, she would call her father to share what she did without violating any security regulations. This was her way of watching tape, like in football. Her dad would give her tips and tricks to make the next missions better for her and those around her. She was a true student as a young Soldier and it showed as she moved through the ranks.

As her first enlistment was ending Ranger School opened up to Females. The first ones who made it through were Officers who were given the time to train and given publicity for making it through. She requested the opportunity and in 2015 she became one of the first enlisted females to graduate. She then put her sights on the Female Engagement Team (FET) program. She applied, went through the interview process and the 26-day selection process, where she rocked it. She read up on the history of these type elements and wanted to ensure she was the best she could be. In 2003 in Ramadi, Iraq, the first team was established. It was named Team Lioness. The members were selected from within the Brigade operating there at the time and literally could be called the plank bearers for this program for all to emulate. One tour as a team member and she was back to the states where again she was promoted. She was selected to lead this team of four due to her leadership abilities.

When they returned to the CoP Bull let Cali brief Hollywood on all the items found and where it leads to. She was very thorough, and this started target packaging for the team moving forward.

The first target was going to be the person identified by the local elder as the money person. This is Abdul Khan, and he is loyal to the Taliban. The elder did not inform the team where he lived precisely but gave a close enough spot where they could cordon the block and clear houses.

Bourne did the intelligence linking to figure out where the most likely places to find Khan would be. Switch laid out the communications plan and Tex gave a weapons brief for the entire team. Bull provided geographic references to the area for all avenues of approach.

Then they waited for higher headquarters to approve air assets and ultimately the raid before commencing. In the meantime, they rehearsed movement techniques to ensure they all were on the same sheet of music. This was another surprise for the enablers. Most had deployed before with other teams and would just sit around all day while waiting to move out. Now they were involved in the planning and rehearsals, true members of the team, not just t-shirt wearers.

It took nearly a day for headquarters to come back with a support package and gave the green light to start the mission. It was going to be a 0200 sp with time on target by 0330.

The team got into the trucks and rolled to a drop-off point for all the dismounted movement. The trucks and drivers were going to move in sets of three to opposite sides of the target block. The walkers split into two groups and moved towards the target.

Once they were within 500 meters, they went to just hand signals the rest of the way. The vehicles were rolling without lights. As both teams got within the 200-meter circle a click of the radio told them to move in. They were going to hit two distinct buildings that were located in nearly identical compounds at the same time.

They knew that all plans go out the window at first contact however, they were hopeful the element of surprise would allow for execution without audibles. At nearly the same exact second both compounds were breached. And the teams spilled in to clear and find the high-value target (HVT). Like most compounds in Afghanistan, these two also had many rooms and outbuildings to go through.

The first compound to the east was being cleared by a Team led by Hollywood and they met resistance pretty quickly. The first shots fired were by two of the FET members on his team and they removed the threat immediately. They were shot at first after they passed an open area in the compound, and they quickly maneuvered to act. All radioed in ok, and they continued through the compound.

Hollywood radioed over to the other compound to Bull. He told him they have taken some contact and moving forward. Bull replied all quiet on the western front. His team continued to clear and found nothing of interest until the last building close to the eastern wall. They entered and Tex stepped on a floorboard that quickly displaced causing him to slide down. He quickly realized he was in a man-made room and called for assistance. JDAM one of the JTACS was right behind him and jumped in to help. The two of them were below the surface and securing a foothold there. Bull and the others cleared the rest of the room and called the east team to tell them all above-ground buildings were complete, and they were moving to subterranean (SUB-T) at this time.

SUB-T is a dangerous concept and was perfected during the Vietnam war by the Vietcong. They would dig tunnel systems to move mass amounts of troops and equipment without the Americans knowing and they have the element of surprise on their side. These tunnels would also have booby traps in them to cause severe damage to any invaders. This was a huge issue for the far superior American Army but has led to training on how to fight in that environment since.

Lucky for this team Tex and Switch had been sent to SUB-T training a year before this. Bull along with the other JTAC Lightspeed, another team member Luke (love of Star Wars) created a secure point at the tunnel entrance while Tex and Switch led the clearing of it.

In the eastern compound, the fire had picked up in volume and Hollywood was still calling in sitreps. They had met resistance in all but one building so far. The entire team is still whole and pushing towards the last three buildings. They have seven prisoners and at least a dozen enemies killed. Bull called into the security platoon and told them to push two vehicles to that compound for security.

As soon as he finished his radio call the burst of machine-gun fire started in the tunnel. Tex had uncovered a complete barracks of fighters and they were in a fight. A second call was made to the security forces to drive the remaining two trucks right into the western compound and park outside the building. Once in place, Bull and the other two jumped down to go into the fight.

The fight was on both sides of the tunnel as those engaging this team were now fleeing to try and escape to the east where they were meeting Hollywood and his team. After forty minutes of a very intense firefight, it was eerily quiet. And both teams cleared towards each other. They found maps drawn on the walls of other US compounds in the area along with Afghan Security forces uniforms and boxes of weapons. They also found American gear that was likely what was taken after the previous team was ambushed. There were three M4s with all attachments on them to include scopes.

This all angered this team more than anything. They were lied to by their own people and were now on a mission to find out how bad it really was. They called in follow-on detainee collection forces to come to collect the targets they were done with and moved out...

CHAPTER 8

Waverly

Bull took in everything during the war but now seemed to drift to other periods of his life. This time he was sitting on his cot but really in his hometown. He was remembering sitting in his favorite watering hole, The Waverly Tavern. He would sit there with his brothers and just drink and forget about the challenges of life. They could sit at this bar for hours and just hang out.

Most times their oldest brother would order some sort of shots trying to kill them, but it was a challenge they all lived for. Their father would join them on occasions and give stories of the old days along with valuable wisdom. This was always accompanied by pizza and more beer.

The oldest brother Elijah was a local legend. He would walk in the bar, and it was like Norm walking into Cheers. He had a prescribed chair and people would move for him at all times. It was weird for Bull to come home and be in this bar after the war started. Before he left it was no issue to sit and drink all day. Once he started making more and more trips across the pond life changed.

He remembers the first time coming home after a trip to the sandbox. He was asked how it felt to fight for oil and lost his shit. Bull went for nearly 7 years without really wanting to go back to his hometown due to this stupid comment.

Their father Tom did not like it and told them all to get off of their shit. He was a big believer in getting over yourself and still is to the current times with all of them. His wisdom coupled with all of his friends who served in Vietnam should have shaped the boys, but being pigheaded runs in the family,

Bull's head stayed here for a while. He remembered sitting with the family and eating meals in the Waverly. Mom would get something small or a soup and a Coors Light. While being a feisty city woman, she had her simple ways that set her apart from all others in the room. While she may have been small in stature, all the children stood in awe and fear of her.

When the Waverly became the place to go for the family, Bull was already well into his career and not really a part of the selection. He did however enjoy a good beer and fun times at a bar. Jameson was always a favorite starter shot. But the memories kept Bull sitting at the bar just remembering how the simple life once was. He too was a simple person with no real big needs. He wanted to make sure he lived life to the fullest at all times. While living it he also wanted to ensure he was making the right choices. He believed this was why he would go through memory lane all the time. It kept him grounded in reality by linking him to his past.

He knew there would always be a Waverly somewhere and it would have to do when he did not travel home. He also felt the need to keep the tradition of camaraderie his brothers and he had alive through trips to other Waverly's around the world. A superstition he held close was that before deployment, they must gather together and drink a ton of liquor and celebrate what may be their last time ever being able to do it. On the flip side, he felt whoever made it home, owed it to all others to do the same upon return or they would be set up for failure.

CHAPTER 9

Solace

After missions everyone had routines. They cleaned weapons, brushed sights reloaded ammo, and inspected their kit. This was all automatic for the team. Once they had their go bag refilled and the kit reassembled, they would go into their own rituals. Bull had a tendency of going to a quiet area and reflect on the day's events. He was not alone. Hollywood would often go on the roof of one of the buildings with a notebook and write for at least an hour about what he thought should have happened and how it actually went down.

Bull would select a corner where no light was and sit in the silence of his thoughts. This allowed him to do the same thing as Hollywood without writing it down. It made him think through each moment of the mission and give himself a play-by-play of each moment as it happened. Of course, each of their perspectives was just that. It would not be until a team meeting a few hours after the mission that all the team would sit together and share their notes to get the entire picture correct.

Many teams and units did this immediately after a mission as a group. It was often called a "Hot Wash". Hollywood was always looking for ways to make the information dump better and he found that giving the team private time for no more than three hours after completion allowed for less adrenaline-fueled remarks and more clarity.

The entire team embraced this as it gave them "me" time after a fight. Finding peace in the chaos was something this team performed well. When they returned to the table after a period of Solace, they would be able to have frank discussions about what they each did well and what they could do better.

The enablers were not used to this and found it amazing not to have to rush into it. They caught on to the principle of letting the adrenaline drain before conducting this. Yet another thing that set this team apart from others. Going against the grain helped them to become the strong team they are. Continuing to practice these little nuances pushed them to even greater success.

Cali found the practice calming for her and the team. Her way of finding peace was throwing weights around. So, once she finished her equipment, she went to the makeshift gym and put in work. For the entire time, you could hear plates clanging. Her workouts were intense and always invited others to try them with her. After missions though, she chose this as her place for peace and reflection. What could she learn from today's mission? Her team was trained well. They conducted many training scenarios at altitudes with heavy rucks on. This allowed them to have stamina in this harsh environment. She tried to recollect every radio call during the fight and take mental notes as she was doing squats.

JDAM enjoyed music, so he would take out his Gibson guitar and strum while he wrote notes of the mission. What could he do better in the future was his first sentence. Not the usual what went well. He always wanted to represent the Air Force as the best liaison possible. This was his way of showing he knew there was always room for improvement while providing actionable feedback to the entire team. He enjoyed the welcoming atmosphere of this team and how they allowed everyone to be part of the fight and not just label them as enablers.

CHAPTER 10

Escape

Mind floats are not uncommon while in a downtime situation for many women and men while at war. They have adrenaline highs and then they crash. When they crash, it is a hard fall. After operating for numerous years, it is easier to get ready for the crash if you plan it out. For some this is a near mirror of what they do during post operations. For others it is a totally different game of tricking your mind.

This is where the float comes in. Teachers and probably medical professionals will call it daydreaming. This is something that truly helps to wind down and find your happy place. Cali would focus on her next workout in the immediate aftermath of the operation. Past that it was more on thinking deeply about the future. Where does she want to settle when she is done with her time in uniform? How will she make it from this point in Afghanistan to a point where she will be a totally different person. She knows she wants to open her own gym. This is a two-part goal as it will benefit her to have her own workout space and provide an income while also allowing her to help others achieve their goals in fitness. She loves children, however, does not have any plans for them in the near or distant future. She likes to spoil her nieces and nephews then send them on their way. So, she floats deep into entrepreneur life. Building her first box in a not-so-urban or rural area but a nice mix of both. She also sees herself as a motivator for others. This adds to the float a chance to mentor youth and fellow veterans as they go through life changes. This is a portion she is torn on. In her mind she sees both existing in the same place. However, she knows not all will want to go to the gym to get motivated. She is always drifting into sleep when more ideas fill her head, and she crashes. Being a determined person, she wakes up and writes everything she remembers of her float in her journal so she can reference it all later.

Bourne tended to float away to his extremely happy place. He loved the water. Growing up on an island tends to help fuel that. When he got into the Army, he was introduced to floating down the rivers in the south. He found his happy place. As he would drift, it would be him on his kayak, with his dog rex and floating down any river he could imagine. He would see himself on the mighty Mississippi many times, even though he never has seen it in person. This was a ritual for him, and he always had rex with him on every journey during his crashing period.

Tex enjoyed hunting, fishing and generally anything outdoors. His float would take him to a huge ranch. On this ranch he would see himself riding a horse with his rifle in a sleeve, he would keep a pack on with essentials and a collapsible fishing rod. This was in case he ventured into any waterways and needed to get some food. He also would make these into adventures that would last well into weeks on end in his mind. It could be from watching too many westerns as a kid or he just had a huge imagination.

Bull tended to drift deep into his own life. He would go all the way back to when he was five to think about his favorite toys like the green machine big wheel he had. That thing was the hotness back then and he could get high speeds on it while also spinning around on it like no one's business. He would also think about the times that were not enjoyable. This was not to make himself sad or angry. It was to try and remember what people did in those situations. He remembered when his grandfather passed. His aunts became crazed with taking possessions. When his other grandfather passed it was a little different but still a splintering of the family. He took mental notes at the time and was determined not to do those things as he evolved. There was a time and place for everything and swooping in during death is not it.

He learned these lessons without knowing it over time. Now as he goes through his adrenaline crashes, he constantly has a movie in his head of the things he has seen in his life. They are vibrant and full-length films that he must process to tell if they are really what he thinks happened at those times in his life. He always comes back to the fact while life is chaos and complicated, he truly is a simple guy who does things.

CHAPTER 11

Warfighting

The team came out of their downtime to sit in on the daily intelligence briefs and find out their next target. Hollywood was summoned to the base secure facility and took Bourne with him. The rest of the team sat and digested everything that was put out. This included all the items they got from exploitation efforts on the last target.

The targeting officer briefed that they uncovered a much larger element than was previously thought to be there. The leader of the cell they encountered was a senior member of the Haqqani network, with ties to both Taliban and ISIS forces in the area. He has not given actionable targets but the hard drives they found have. The team will be splitting into two like they have been. This time however, they will have a mountain separating them which may be an added risk for quick reaction elements.

Hollywood stepped away after the initial brief at headquarters. He was succumbed by the magnitude of what this team had fallen into. The team they replaced was so messed up that they did not realize the enemy presence, nor their operational status in the area. He removed himself due to his anger at the last team leader. How could this dude brief this as an all-calm area? How could he say they had no issues? How could he not brief what happened just before the switch out?

Bull was just planning. He stood with the team and asked what their thoughts were. How did they want to split for this mission? He knew Cali wanted to be on the most dangerous side of the mission, so asked her which one she wanted? She chose to stay on his team this time. This was surprising as his side was the least likely side for a fire fight. He then looked to the other enablers since he was shocked now. They stayed the course with what they have done in the past.

Hollywood came back in, and Bull briefed him on what the teams would look like while also letting him know the two paths they would take to accomplish the mission. Hollywood was a bit detached, still angry at the previous team and digesting everything he just heard. Of course, he supported what Bull came up with so that would not be an issue. He wanted Bourne to get a brief together for the team, so they all knew what they were truly facing. The data he just received prior had made his mind explode. He now wanted the entire team to hear this,

Bourne did not like to half ass anything. He took the data that was given to him and went to his hooch. He told Hollywood to give him an hour to give a proper brief. He might have been as angry as Hollywood while making this thing right.

Hollywood told the team to be back for a full brief in one hour.

They re-assembled and were all ready to hear what the mission set would be. With three different maps on screens and terrain model set up in the middle of the room. (Terrain models are a built-up representation of what the area looks like based off of imagery and intelligence) While most operations centers will have this type of set-up it is not common for small teams to have all of this set up for a mission. As Hollywood and the team have shown, they are not common. This was a basic set for them. Once Hollywood gave a warning order to the main members, he expected high level critical thinking from every member of the unit. He spread this to the enablers the day he met each of them. It was like a virus but this time it was for good.

In most operations cells the junior enlisted Soldiers are given the task of preparing all the maps and terrain models for the senior leaders. They then are in the shadows as the brief goes on and might get a challenge coin for a job well done. On this team all members are expected to know the entire mission and build the briefs. It made zero sense to the Team, the conventional way of doing it. This made every member know the exact mission from start to finish and started the thinking part of it.

CHAPTER 12

The Brief

Hollywood came in and gave the overview of the mission, this provided a great one over the world verbalization of what this team would be doing in the next 48 hours. He detailed who would be on which team by name and expected timelines tracking back to 20 minutes after this brief is over.

Bourne was up next, and his part was extremely important. He had to use the maps, terrain model and intelligence to explain what the enemy forces are expected to be made up of. He also had to provide the most dangerous and most likely scenarios that the enemy might attempt when they are faced with their force coming at them. The most dangerous for the enemy would be to hit the team prior to making it to the objective. This would take them out of their security zone and leave them vulnerable to maneuver by the ground force commander that would lead to the enemy taking heavy losses.

The most likely scenario was based on the tactics the enemy has been employing throughout the region and in this war. Bourne emphasized this one. He told the team to expect hidden caches in the target area for the enemy to maneuver to so they could bring fire from anywhere. He also told them that outside of the secure zone there would be improvised explosive devices spread out to slow movement in. He went over the forecast for the next 72-96 hours so the team could be prepared for environmental concerns. He then called up Cali to brief on the villages in the area of both targets.

She had a very detailed brief on the makeup of each of the villages. She gave elders names and descriptions of specific structures in each one. She and her team did extensive research once they had an inkling of where the mission was going. She then passed it off to JDam to brief pre planned targets and planned air support that would be on hand for the mission.

JDam highlighted both villages as off limits for targeting due to proximity of civilians and collateral damage. He gave everyone a free shot if they knew no civilians were in a building then it could be targeted. His team would also be handling all joint fires, so the planned targets were very important for the mission.

CHAPTER 13

Higher Headquarters

In the south of Afghanistan other teams were operating. A few were utilizing their enablers the way this team was. As it has been established Hollywood was a different type of leader and the team was better for it. The southern teams ran into a serious issue on the night of the last mission. That would be the second major incident for enablers of a team in the last month plus.

This team was operating in Panjwai in Kandahar Province. They were on a mission and instead of leading the charge had the enablers kicking in doors and clearing rooms. On this last mission they ran into a strong Taliban force and half of the enablers were wounded with 3 being killed.

This led the senior leaders in the operations space to pause and think about standards of utilization. The General in charge of the teams had to answer to the pentagon and in turn the media for this disaster down in the south. He was no longer willing to use enablers mixed with the teams, at least not for the next few weeks.

The word trickled through the layers of commands and finally to Chowkay. Hollywood got a call on his burner to reach back to command on a secure line. He ran out and got on the comms. He threw his watch cap across the room as he was told what happened and what he must comply with.

He charged out of the room and attempted to gain his composure. He walked around the small CoP for ten minutes before heading back into the brief back room. He opened the door, and all eyes were on him. They all could tell something was terribly wrong.

He explained what happened to the team in Kandahar. He then proceeded to let them know the mission they had just laid out would have to be changed 100%. He would only be able to take nine people onto the initial move to target and they all had to be core team members.

Picking the members would not be hard as they all know their role and will be willing to fill any area of the mission. He tapped Bourne to be the senior guy left back along with Switch and Bob. All of the enablers were staying back with them and would be divided up into two teams with one operator and the rest filled with them as two separate QRF elements.

The enablers were not happy with HQs decision at all as they have become part of this team, part of this family. Although unhappy, they supported Hollywood and planned for actions if needed.

CHAPTER 14

Back on the Hill

Bull now in charge and Justice taking immediate control of the vicinity with the others who were not wounded. He had the four enablers who came up on the Pedro bird and Luke from the team with him. He sent Cali and Luke to sweep the east and JDam and Spirit to check the west while him and Outlaw searched enemy in the center for documents and intel.

Doc was frantic getting all the wounded treated. He had three in dire need of further medical care. Hollywood was in the worst shape and told Doc to care for the others first. They had two options to get them out. The healthy team members could carry them all down to the spot Bull and Justice found or try to guide in a bird under possible fire up on the mountain.

Justice and the others completed the sweep and reported back. He did not even think twice he took them back out and created a hasty landing zone and shot the coordinates to Bull.

They called in for a medevac with an escort bird to ensure they were able to make it all the way in.

With time ticking away and every second beating into their heads they waited. It was not patiently at all. It was the longest 15 minutes ever waiting on this miracle flight to come in. The radio chirped and Angel 16 was on approach. The pilot said they would not touch the ground, but just hover for them to be ready to load and unload rapidly.

As Angel 16 came into view Justice popped red smoke and had all the casualties to the left of the smoke. As the bird came to a hover four people jumped off the right side and they loaded the four casualties. The bird was not there for more than a minute and gone again.

The four that got off were Switch, Bob and two more of the enablers. The team now had 12 members. The four members who just came up also had bags of ammo, water some food and more medical supplies. Bull called them all in for a huddle and they planned the final assault on the original objectives. They were still 2 kilometers away. They decided to wait till midnight to move out. It was now 1930 and they had been at it since just before midnight the day before. Justice implemented a work rest plan so they could keep guards up and get some rest while also refitting gear on the go.

Bull took this time to sit and reflect. He could taste iron in his mouth from the smell of blood everywhere. He also had it all over his uniform. The heavy scent of cordite sat in the haze that became the mountain top now. Again, he paused to let it sink in and look over the vast country and think to himself, "If I was not fighting in a war, this would be a beautiful country".

CHAPTER 15

Midnight on the Mountain

The team got out of the fog and the last guards Bull and Justice, woke everyone up. Each remember checked their gear and had someone else check them to ensure they had everything. While on that last shift, Bourne radioed with heart dropping news. Hollywood and Tex both succumbed to their wounds while on the operating table in Bagram. They took the time while everyone else was asleep to go through their own emotions and get set for the mission. They also knew they had to tell everyone once they were alert enough to comprehend the message.

They asked Bourne what happened to the QRF that was coming to help them during the fight. This was a hot subject, especially with the news of Hollywood and Tex. Bourne told them, as they were ascending the mountain, they were coming from the opposite side of the mountain where the team climbed. Their commander did not look at the intelligence assessment of that approach and this proved costly. They were stopped in their tracks by a large force that was embedded on the lower to mid side of the mountain in small villages. They just got out of that fight less than an hour before this radio call. It was a huge error, and many Soldiers were wounded during the fight. This added to the adrenaline already pumping through their bodies.

Bull gathered everyone around a large rock on the top of the mountain. He broke the news as gently as one could in this situation. He told them, despite herculean efforts by Doc and each one of you we couldn't keep them with us. We now must go out and keep a level head while finishing this portion of the operation to kill or capture the leader of the network in this area. They were also briefed on the situation with the QRF for complete transparency. He then gave them each ten minutes to go off and digest it and get their game face back on.

They got in a staggered column and moved towards the objective. There was not time to mourn right now. They must compartmentalize everything and move on until the time was right.

CHAPTER 16

Strategic Thinking

Knowing he was down to just over half of his team Bull was thinking forward. Just before they moved out, he radioed Bourne again. He requested replacements for the two lost to be activated and sent from Bagram to their location. He knew there were two young operators on station that had worked out with the team a few times and requested them by name. He requested Irish Whiskey and Puka Puka.

The message was relayed to group headquarters and Bourne would relay their response when he received it.

Bull did something here no team leader had done before. He put an enabler at the point, leading the movement to the objective. Justice took the northern flank with switch while Bob and Luke took the southern flank as sniper overwatch. Cali was put in the position of leader in the wedge movement. She was fired up from what had transpired and relished the role.

One kilometer to into the movement and Spirit halted

them. He called Cali up and showed her what he saw. The enemy was entrenched from the west, and they could see Hesco Bastions that were stolen from bases throughout the country filled and double stacked. (HESCOs are large wire surrounded canvas lined containers filled with dirt to create a barrier against small arms and RPG fire) The enemy used intelligence gathered from watching the Americans to fortify their position.

Cali saw this and knew it would be a suicide mission to bring the team in with only 12 people. They would need at least a company size element to cause damage to the fortress. She radioed Bull and told them to collapse on her. When the team arrived, they all saw a daunting task ahead of them. This team is truly resilient and has a forward-thinking mindset. They again assumed a tight perimeter and made suggestions on how to tackle this.

To the east of the compound was a village with at least twenty dwellings, tightly packed in with two crossroads and at least a dozen shops. To the south was another 15 to twenty dwellings spread out with dirt paths between them like a scene out of Vietnam. On the north side was mostly woods and a couple flocks of goats and sheep with their handlers. This truly was the rock and hard place for the team.

The first thing off the table was the airstrikes due to the dwellings and proximity of the base. The team took an hour to come up with the best-case scenario. This was for them to slowly surround the compound with overwatch positions and conduct recon while awaiting a larger force to come in from the west along the path they did. Once they arrived the unit commander would be given all the pertinent data to execute and assault on the compound.

The assault force was going to be led by an Army unit that was enroute to take over for the qrf unit that got decimated in the previous mission. They pivoted and started their move up to link in with the team. They are also bringing the two team replacements up with them.

CHAPTER 17

New Dudes

Irish Whiskey

Being new to a unit is one thing, being a replacement for those we have lost is totally different and he knew this. He knew he had to be his best self and morph into the unit once he caught up to them. As Jameson jumped into the patrol out, he always said a quick prayer for the entire unit. He was a devout Christian. He also happened to be one of the best trackers and navigators any of the senior members of his team had ever met. He was born in Murfreesboro, Arkansas with a population of less than 2,000. The youngest of four, he also was the only son. He attended Murfreesboro Highschool in Pike County, just like the rest of his family before him. He participated in nearly every sport the school had to offer. On the football field, he was the middle linebacker, and he was ferocious when he met a ball carrier. He ran anchor in the 4x 400 on his track team and always had a huge smile on his face.

Jameson's grandmother owned a local restaurant The

Down South Dine. Everyone knew Mrs. Wilson (Tracy) and they loved to congregate in her establishment. Her fried bologna and potato salad is to die for. When tourists come to town to try and find diamonds in the local dig site, the economy of the town skyrockets along with the population. The restaurant sits just off the main square of the city in this quaint old southern town.

He was also the first and only grandson in the line of children Tracy's children had. When he decided, he did not want to go to college right away, but rather join the Army, it broke their hearts. Tracy and Jameson's mother Helen were scared for him. They went to the local church, the Murfreesboro Church of Christ, and asked the women's group to help them pray on their thoughts. After a few hours of prayer, pie, and coffee the ladies realized that Jameson was following his path, the one the Lord laid out for him.

His first stop for training was at Fort Benning, Georgia. This is the home of the Infantry and now the maneuver center of excellence. It sits near Columbus Georgia and is mere miles from the state line with Alabama. Like in athletics and in academics, Jameson excelled in basic training and advanced individual training. His Drill Sergeants took notice of his capabilities and pushed him harder. He graduated at the top of his class and was sent directly to Airborne School instead of a duty assignment. This also proved not to be a task for him as he graduated with no issues. He then got his orders to report to the 3rd Battalion 75th Ranger Regiment right there on Fort Benning. This was a dream assignment for a young Infantryman.

He got settled in under the tutelage of great young noncommissioned officers (NCOs). He made it through the indoctrination process and became a rifleman in the 2nd squad of the 3rd platoon Alpha company. He called Murfreesboro every night to tell his mom how his day was and that he was fine. Some of the guys made fun of him for always calling but he took it in stride.

He was in the unit less than a year before they felt he was ready to attend Ranger School (The United States Army Ranger School is a 62-day small unit tactics and leadership course that develops functional skills directly related to units whose mission is to engage the enemy in close combat and direct-fire battles. Ranger training was established in September 1950 at Fort Benning, Georgia). Once again Jameson laid the hammer down and went true blue through the course.

Jameson was promoted to Sergeant in under two years. He was a team leader and very good at it. He was sent to sniper school and again he rocked it. He was having the time of his life in this unit. He also was becoming a little bored. He asked to go to more schools, and they obliged. He went to Pathfinder, Air Assault, HALO, and SERE. Even though he was on a great trajectory, he still called home daily to let Helen and Tracy know he was good and still performing at an optimal level and still going to church on base every week.

When he came up for reenlistment, Jameson decided he wanted a new challenge and applied for Special Forces Assessment and Selection. He trained hard for it and once his date came, he hopped on his Hayabusa and sped up to Fort Bragg in Fayetteville, North Carolina. Once again, this Soldier faced an amazing challenge and was selected. He rode back to Benning and processed out to move to Bragg for his qualification course as a weapons sergeant.

He graduated from the Q course and was assigned to a Special Forces Group. This is where he became a member of the team, he is currently running point for Team 99875.

Puka Puka

When Jameson got to Fort Campbell, he became fast friends with Alberto, who was also new to the team. Alberto and Jameson would hang out after work hours nearly every day. The rest of the team had been together for the better part of four years. The only reason slots opened on the team, was due to two old guys retiring. Both of these young guns cherished the opportunity to be on one of the most storied teams of this group. They also knew they needed to be tight knit with each other to fight off any hijinks from the old hats.

Alberto was born and raised in Aguadilla Pueblo, Puerto Rico, a northwestern town on the island with beautiful beaches, alongside his tight-knit family. He attended Juan Suarez Pelegrina High School located in the Montana Barrio. The school had less than a thousand total students enrolled, and everyone knew each other.

While growing up he was the middle of five children and second of three boys. His older siblings both played basketball and ran track in High School. He decided he would go with basketball and baseball. His older brother followed their father into the National Guard, his sister went to the University of Puerto Rico, Aguadilla campus.

He decided after he finished with basketball and baseball in high school, it was time for a change. He wanted to be like their grandfather and join the active Army as a medic. So, during his senior year he went to the recruiter and asked what he had to do to become a Soldier and a medic. The recruiter told him everything he would be responsible to do before he would be allowed to ship out.

Despite playing sports in high school, he still wasn't in the best shape. He asked his father and grandfather for advice, and they readily handed it to him. They wanted him to start the next morning before sunrise with long runs. His first day was just two miles, but it was much harder than he thought it would be.

Alberto decided he needed to get serious. He started hitting the roads at five in the morning and was able to get comfortable running for long distances. He would then go and work out with anything he could find around their property. He had 6 weeks to get ready for basic and every minute was devoted to getting better.

He was taught early that a journey is just the means to finish a goal in life. He knew if he chased this goal the journey would be amazing, and he would be fulfilled. He did not want to let anyone down, especially not his grandparents. His grandmother was a very strong woman, and she shared her views with all the grandchildren. She also was an awesome cook, so she was always feeding him. Of course, he enjoyed eating her food, but he knew he would have to work harder to enjoy it. This motivated him to work harder to be the best.

As the time was drawing near to ship out, Alberto was getting butterflies in his stomach. He did not want to let anyone down; he did not want to let himself down. He did know he trained like a beast for the last couple months. The early mornings and late nights were definitely working, he could see it in the mirror, and he felt 100% better.

On Sunday before his ship day his whole family came over for a party to wish him good luck. The food was plentiful and every person who came had brought a huge platter with them. There was definitely enough food to feed an army in the house that day. There was also lots of music as his uncle Manny came with his band and played from the time, they arrived at one in the afternoon until just before midnight.

Staff Sergeant (SSG) Reynaldo Ortiz came and picked up Alberto on Monday morning at just before five in the morning. His mother and grandmother handed SSG Ortiz two big containers of food for him and his team. He then drove him to the military entrance processing station. The day was finally here. As they drove to San Juan, Alberto was asking his final questions.

Alberto: How long is the flight to South Carolina?

SSG Ortiz: Maybe a four-hour total flight time not counting layovers.

Alberto: Will he be able to see the area at all or just train?

SSG Ortiz: You will not have time to tour the area, you will be busy becoming a Soldier.

Alberto: Who will pick me up at the airport?

SSG Ortiz: There will be Soldiers there to pick you up, you will not miss them.

When they arrived SSG Ortiz parked, and they walked into the station. Alberto shook his hand and thanked him for helping him, then walked through double brown doors into a new life. He did not even turn around as he was so excited to start this journey.

That day was long with traveling from Puerto Rico to Columbia, South Carolina with a layover in Atlanta. When you have that much time on your hands your mind races about what was about to happen. Alberto was restless and anxious as he awaited his connection, so he just walked all around Atlanta's Hartsfield-Jackson airport. The layover was two hours, and he was finally on the southwest flight to his last stop.

He arrived at the airport, got his bag, and saw two individuals in uniform standing corralling other young people. He knew he was in the right area and went up to them and asked if they were from Fort Jackson. They looked sternly at him and told him to get over by the others, stand in lone and await the bus.

Now he was asking himself, "What did I get myself into?" As they loaded the bus and were told to be quiet, he just faced forward. They arrived at Fort Jackson at midnight. Two Drill Sergeants got on the bus and welcomed them very calmly. Then went crazy yelling at them to get off the bus. All he thought was "Welcome to the Army".

His time there was fast and furious as the entire group learned what it meant to be a Soldier. He enjoyed marksmanship training as he never shot a rifle before. This piqued his interest into other avenues that may be available for him in the future. He finished his time at basic training and was sent to Fort Sam Houston in Texas to become a medic.

Although he wanted this profession, he was bored with the training. He went through it and passed all exams both in classroom and in a field environment, but he lost his passion for it. He called his grandfather and talked to him many times over the time he was in the course. His grandfather told him to finish up the training get to his first duty station, then work into something else.

He left Fort Sam and headed to Fort Bragg, North Carolina. On the way he was sent to Airborne School which again, helped him in finding his true passion. He saw guys at Fort Benning going through other specialized training at the schoolhouse and around the base.

He thought the Ranger Regiment soldiers were great and wanted to learn more. When he got done with Airborne school, he had three days to explore the base and found himself talking to a Special Forces Recruiter. This is where he realized he knew what he wanted. It would be tough to get to his new unit, drop a packet and then work for it. He would have to wait until he was promoted to Sergeant so maybe a couple of years to train and prepare for it was ahead of him.

He took all the information he could from the recruiter. This included workouts to get his body prepared and books to read so he would understand the fundamental foundation of the Green Berets.

The first book he was told to read was one about a Green Beret Legend. It was "Five Years to Freedom."

When Green Beret Lieutenant James N. Rowe was captured in 1963 in Vietnam, his life became more than a matter of staying alive.

In a Vietcong POW camp, Rowe endured beri-beri, dysentery, and tropical fungus diseases. He suffered grueling psychological and physical torment. He experienced the loneliness and frustration of watching his friends die. And he struggled every day to maintain faith in himself as a soldier and in his country as it appeared to be turning against him.

His survival is testimony to the disciplined human spirit.

His story is gripping.

He wound up reading this book three times. It kept him motivated during his early days at Fort Bragg. The story of LT Rowe motivated Alberto to get promoted ahead of his peers and become a viable candidate to make selection.

CHAPTER 18

Link-UP

The radio chirped as the unit approached from the west spread out over kilometer. The first element that reached Bull and Cali was 2nd platoon and the first squad leader moved forward to conduct link up. Soon two obvious operators moved forward, and it was Irish Whiskey and Puka Puka. Cali pulled out her map and briefed the SL on the plan and where the team wanted the company to array.

Bull greeted the two operators and sent them into a position just to his west so they could provide sniper overwatch from there. All sides of the compound now had great overwatch with 6 teams of two in position. The company would be briefed on the suggested plan based on the recon conducted. The commander took the suggestions and agreed to the course of action. He sent his platoons out three maneuvered to the north with one stopping along with Justice and his overwatch position. The other two would stop just short of the village. One platoon would move into the village upon the start while the other entered the compound. The fourth platoon moved to the south. They would split into squads and clear all the dwellings once the attack started. Bull stayed with the commander short of the western wall with a mortar team. It was around 1600 when everyone got into position.

Understanding they owned the night the commander made the call to wait for dusk to start the final approach and attack.

Tactical patience is of the upmost importance as this will be the culmination of a bad few days. The team was still anguishing inside about their brothers, the company commander was on edge knowing that revenge might be on the hearts of the team and his guys knew a bunch of the guys wounded in the QRF incident. This was a scenario ripe for bad news.

Sundown was at 2015 and as the light turned to dark the command of Tallyho chirped over all radios. Like an orchestra the eastern platoons moved with one in the village and one pushing towards the compound entrance. 2 squads of the southern platoon pushed to the compound while one systematically cleared the dwellings.

The platoon in the north kept one team in a blocking position while everyone else moved on the compound. At exactly 2017 the first volley of mortar rounds started into the center of the compound. Then the first small arms fire started at the eastern entrance. Large volumes of fire were going off on both sides. This posed a problem since all sides could not fire at once without the risk of fratricide.

Justice took his first shot at about the same time. A group of enemy fighters were trying to maneuver around to surround the platoon advancing on them. There were around ten of them. His first shot took out a tall fighter in the center. It was truly an easy target as he was a clear foot taller than the others.

With the blocking position and a second sniper position this ten-man team was taken completely out. The element from the south climbed over the southern wall in a clear surprise shooting as they crested the HESCO. It was about 10 minutes in when a loud explosion rocked the inside of the compound, and the radio went crazy for assistance. The that entered from the east had set off an explosion by accident and had numerous Soldiers down in varying states of need. The commander and his small headquarters element did not panic, they kept orchestrating this attack. Bull told the commander he would take his team straight over the west wall along with Doc and move in to triage and help those Soldiers in there. He agreed and off they went.

The volume of fire had not died down and the commander made the call for the other operators in overwatch positions to move in to help. Bull, Cali, and Doc jumped the HESCO and immediately were met with a barrage of machine gun fire. Luckily, they all were able to get behind cover and return fire on that position which seemed to be in a hut. Justice, Bob, and Switch came in from the north and were met before they reached the wall with an intense amount of fire as well. They quickly realized this compound was more than the recon gave them. It was complex on the inside with more HESCO mazes in there and huts strewn throughout. The fact that they were getting lit up outside from outside made a light go on for Justice. They were moving by underground systems. Luke had JDam maneuver back to the commander's position and help call in laser guided munitions while Outlaw and Spirit were with him. Irish Whiskey and Puka Puka made the move over to the north wall.

The call from Justice explaining that the enemy was underground was eye opening for the command team and the operators. Most of the team had fought in the tunnels just recently, so they started to think they needed to take the fight underground. The new additions after landing over the wall wound up not near Bull and his team. This was due to the complexity of the compound. They quickly realized they were not on the same level as the bottom of the HESCO. When they jumped, they fell much longer than they climbed and were now under the compound and disoriented.

The radio quickly chimed on internal that they thought they were underground and were trying to find their way to the next rooms. Bull told them to drop cookies so they could find them. He did not mean literal cookies but infrared chem lights. They responded with Affirm.

The fighting throughout the compound was still intense on all sides. Justice and his team entered underground from the north. They had already taken out over two dozen fighters by the time they got in there. There were reports of fighting in the eastern village as well now. The Soldiers near the southern dwellings had not found any resistance nor were they finding any signs of fighters.

With most of the fighting in the compound and the east village the commander could not drop any rounds on either due to danger close of his Soldiers and the civilians in the village. It was chaos in both areas when there was another huge explosion from the south side of the compound. It was followed shortly by two more with huge flashes rising skyward. The radios from the platoon on the southside went silent.

CHAPTER 19

Flash and Bang

Cali looked over at the giant fire ball to her right and then back at Bull and Doc. She knew this was bad. The Last they heard was Justice and his team were underground coming from the North. There was a platoon minus clearing the South side of the compound and Whiskey and Puka were underground somewhere over there.

There was an eerie silence for what seemed like forever. Bull waited for a while to see if anyone would radio in. The first to break squelch was the commander asking for a sitrep from that platoon specifically. Again, there was silence.

Bull was staring to the east at a structure in the compound when he saw an IR strobe coming from it. It was Justice and his team emerging with a cloud coming behind them. As they emerged each fell to their knees and moved against the structure for cover. Cali sprinted over to assess and noticed they all had blood on them, and their faces were covered in mud. She gave hand signals back to Bull and Doc telling them they were conscious but banged up. Justice muttered that it had to be hundreds of pounds of explosives in the tunnels.

Cali made Justice, Bob and Switch move out of the compound and back to the commander's area. There the company senior medic could take care of them while they continued to figure out what was left of this element.

Bull and Doc moved toward where the 1st injured Soldiers were believed to be and finally got to triaging them, they grabbed Cali on the way. They radioed back to the commander the status. It was at this moment they all realized there was not any gunfire anymore.

There were thirteen Soldiers who were badly injured in the initial blast on the east side of the compound with two being killed instantly including the squad leader and the 1st platoon leader. The squad that was in the east village moved into the compound and began helping with the wounded and finding places for shelter.

Bull radioed internal to check his team. All answered except Whiskey and Puka. He had Luke and his team start tearing down buildings in the compound to create a LZ. They would need multiple birds to get all the wounded out. JDam and the unit XO came in and started assisting with the LZ. Justice and his team after about twenty minutes, came back in and linked in with Bull.

The team of 6 moved to the south of the compound and found multiple unconscious Soldiers just past a second HESCO barrier. The good news is these 10 were alive. Doc stayed with them, and the rest moved forward trying to find any more.

The movement was slow as they kept encountering trip

wires and pressure plates. The entire compound was rigged to explode somehow.

Even though he was banged up, Justice pushed forward and was disabling every device they found. It took over 90 minutes to go 150 meters.

When they go through the obstacle belt, they had a platoon behind them, and all elements were in the compound now. They reached a crater that was 40 feet wide and 30 feet long. It looked like multiple bombs were dropped on this area. There was no need to hide now so they all went to white light and were yelling out to see if anyone would answer.

The EVAC birds were called for the first group of Soldiers found plus the 10 found unresponsive but alive. A total of twenty-three wounded and two confirmed KIA so far.

CHAPTER 20

Crater

As they slowly climbed down into the crater, they started hearing sounds of life. While still horrible, this meant there were living Soldiers under all this.

The command team radioed up that a total of twenty-seven of his company were still unaccounted for. This told Bull that there were twenty-nine down here. For the moment they knew they would be digging by hand to get them out. Cali yelled out got some. She had been on the eastern side of the crater digging and fell through a pocket of debris. She pulled herself up and yelled have at least seven here. Soldiers ran over and started helping to pull guys out all were banged up, bleeding but all were alive, a great find. They were moved over to the LZ area. The Soldiers who got them out came running back. Cali was joined by Bull and Luke in the hole which was truly the tunnel system now. They continued to move around debris and stack sensitive items so they can grab them on the way out.

Another hour had passed and still twenty Soldiers were missing.

The first three evac birds had come and gone taking out 15 of the wounded.

Justice now is yelling out he found another batch. Bob and Switch were with him now along with Spirit and Outlaw. They all lowered themselves down about 6 feet into the crater. They found most of the rest in this area. There were Soldiers piled on top of one another and they started to pull them apart and attempt to lift them out. The rest of the element arrived at this location. They already found four more KIA in the first pile and three in real bad shape missing limbs and bleeding bad. All had been lifted out with care and carried over to the triage area.

13 left is what the radio chimed.

Bull was in the hole and saw another part of the tunnel to the west of them, so he took three Soldiers with him and moved forward. Justice radioed again got six more out only three were banged up the other three were just trapped.

Seven to go.

After multiple turns in the tunnel Bull found another debris wall. They started pushing, pulling, and ripping all the crap out of their way and one of the Soldier yelled I see helmets. They got a hole big enough to climb through.

The other side of the wall had the smell of explosives and blood and very thick stale air. The push forward was quick as all of them got through the opening. They found three of the Soldiers leaned up against each other sitting back-to-back. They were alive but completely out cold. They all had super-ficial wounds on them and blood on their extremities. Bull sent one of the Soldiers back to get more hands and he came back with six more. They passed the three through the hole and out of the tunnel. Now with 7 in his party Bull pushed forward in the dark tunnel he could see boots about 50 feet ahead and moved quickly to them.

There was a Soldier on his back, no helmet on and his wounds already dressed. He was alert and told them the team guys helped him and went to find his buddy and pointed the direction.

The wounded Soldier was taken out of the tunnel and with five in his party they pressed forward. They made a couple more turns and found the remaining three. The PL from the link up was seated against a wall missing his lower left leg and right arm but alive. He had tourniquets on him and writing on his head and leg telling times for the medical staff. He nodded towards the other two and said they saved him before he passed out.

Bull ran over to the last two. And it was Whiskey with his hand in a grip on Puka's set as if he was pulling him to safety but they both were gone. They saved that entire set of Soldiers before dying from their wounds.

CHAPTER 21

Sunrise

The rising sun painted a horrible picture. There were enemy bodies everywhere in and around the compound. The evac birds just lifted off with the last of the eight killed in action in this fight.

Bull gathered up his team and they took a knee, bowed their heads, and had a moment of clarity in what they had been through the last few days. A total of seven evacuated wounded and four killed in action. Two of which, were on their very first operation.

The company commander came over and stood with Bull with the sun silhouetting them. It was a surreal moment for everyone else as they saw these two leaders, who were completely drained each with a hand on the other's shoulder with the rising sun behind them.

Bull came back and made sure everyone was good. He told them the commander thanked them for their herculean efforts to save his men. He also let them know it was time to collect the intel and get out of there.

They went into the remaining structures that were standing and took everything they could, labeled the bags, put all items in three body bags and threw them on the last bird picking up the company guys. The team would descend on foot.

They did not have to do this, they wanted to do this. They have been through hell and back in 72 hours lost 4 good dudes and 7 more wounded bad enough to be evacuated. Only 1 of the 10 remaining would not be receiving a Purple Heart after all of this. They changed his name from Luke to Lucky.

It took them 15 hours to descend safely and get to the original pick-up point. Here a Chinook from the Minnesota national Guard landed and picked them up. The air crew handed out bottles of water to the team as they got on.

CHAPTER 22

Red Wine

They landed on CoP Red Wine and were met by Bourne and the rest of the enablers. Bourne briefed Bull on the status of the pack up of the personal belongings for the four KIA. He told them everything was packed and ready to be shipped back to their families, all sensitive items were in lock boxes, and they had orders to pack all of their stuff for refit back to Bagram.

A back-up team was flown from the states as soon as the first fight started and by the time they landed, the call was made to send them into replace.

No team member wanted to be replaced, they felt they needed to finish their tour right there at Red Wine. Higher Headquarters believed they saw more combat than any team in the last couple years and needed to refit and possibly re-deploy.

CHAPTER 23

Bagram

Two days had passed since the team arrived back at Bagram. Headquarters set up a memorial for the four warriors lost in the mountains of Kunar. The 48 hours since they landed were filled with debriefs and working out at the gym and around the airfield. They all took time to shower and eat a couple hot meals. This always helps when trying to deal with adversity. All of the wounded team members were in Germany at Landstuhl already. They were receiving world class care, preparing them for the journey back to the States. Bull had talked to all of the injured members families via satellite phone over the last two days. He also spoke with the families of those who would be memorialized in the next few hours.

This is not a job any leader cherishes. This is a job that hurts deep to the core. With each click of the phone Bull felt life drain from him but new he had to get right back on it for the next family. He wanted to be the one who called instead of some random Army person handling it from the home.

It was 1030 on a Tuesday and Bull and Bourne walked out to the memorial area. They walked up to their brother's boots and helmets with their weapons stabbed down through them and nodded to each one of them. They then took their place up in the front of the set-up area to the side of the podium facing where the crowd would be.

The adrenaline in them was pumping like on a mission. Cali led the rest of the team up to the front row facing the display and the podium. Directly to the front of the speakers was seating for the distinguished guests. This would be the commander of the region of Afghanistan, the commander of Special Operations in Afghanistan all the Command Sergeants Major who were in the area and partner forces leadership.

These were definitely more for the audience then for those who knew them personally. It was and is a time-honored tradition in the service. It also has grown way out of its intended purpose.

CHAPTER 24

Eulogy

A junior Lieutenant (LT)was given the inauspicious duty of running the ceremony.

LT: Ladies and Gentlemen the ceremony will start in five minutes.

Soft music plays in the background as everyone in attendance finds their seats. There is a dead calm in the air. The team members only are staring straight ahead sort of in a zombie state. The distinguished guests shake each other's hands and exchange pleasantries.

LT: Please find you seats the ceremony will begin in 3 minutes.

Those 180 seconds take a lifetime the members facing the audience from the podium area are stoic, looking like statues.

LT: 1 Minute till the ceremony begins

A C-17 takes off in the background, breaking the silence. The team in the front row and the podium members do not flinch. Many in the crowd look around to see the plane.

LT: Ladies and Gentlemen thank you for taking a part of your busy schedule to pay homage to these warriors who gave the ultimate sacrifice here in battle. Understand we are still in a war zone and there will be outside noises, so please remain cognizant of that a respect those we are here for.

This was the first time Bull and Bourne actually looked up since they did not know the LT and did not expect anything like this to come out of his mouth. This was the first time broke their statuesque stance in front of the audience.

LT: Pleas rise for the invocation by Chaplain Jersey

Chaplain Jersey: On behalf of the leadership of the Group Colonel Newcomb and CSM Figtan Good Morning fellow servicemen and women and distinguished guests' thanks for being with us today. Let us pray.

The Lord is my shepherd, I shall not want.

As these men received the mission, they did not question their mortality, they worked on the problem in front of them. Hollywood, Tex, Jameson, and Puka all were highly motivated men, and all pushed forward where others would have faltered.

He makes me lie down in green pastures, he leads us through quiet waters, he clears our souls. Yea, though I walk through the valley of the shadow of death, I will fear no evil: for thou art with me; your rod and your staff they comfort me.

You prepare a table before me while in the presence of our enemy: you anoint my head with oil and my cup runs over.

Surely goodness and mercy shall follow me all the days of my life: and I will dwell in the house of the Lord forever.

These men are forever in your care oh Lord for the kingdom, the power and glory are yours, now and forever.

Amen

LT: Group Commander

Col Newcomb: Thank you Chaplain Jersey. Distinguished guests, Group Soldiers and other servicemembers we are here to remember those we have lost. I remember when Hollywood arrived at group just out of the Q course. The Standard at the time was to place the new officers into the Group or BN staff sections while they wait on a team. He sat before me and the executive officer full of confidence and full of pure desire. We had already researched him and knew his stats from his platoon leadership time. He was a rock star.

Thirty minutes into our chat with him, he said sir, I understand this is a feeling out process and I know you have all the information on me as it was handed to you. I have studied this group from the moment I was given my marching orders to report here. You have a storied career sir, I am honored to be here, I do not want to rot in staff but understand the line of succession that is in place. If you could just give me my responsibilities for now, I will knock them out of the box, and you will have no choice but to find a way to put me on a team.

I was quiet for a second or two and nodded my head. This young officer just showed me the size of his cajones and the sheer amount of confidence he had. I told him, he would have a team as quick as we could make it happen and sent him to the air section.

Tex was as humble as he was proud to be a Green Beret and a Soldier, he always asked what he could do for his country and laughed as he walked away from me. I always told him to keep his giant truck out of my lot, now I wish I could still see it.

Jameson and Puka were two young studs, two young men who were guided by great upbringing and mentors. They both arrived around the same time if memory serves me correctly. We did a newcomer breakfast and training session. I tell you what, I knew I was not young anymore, but these two made me look like I was in a home pushing my wheelchair and had zero mercy on me. This is why I sent them forward on this deployment as reserves and ultimately to this team.

Our business is not for the faint at heart. We know when we join that there will be an end date either through the expiration of our contract, retirement or making the ultimate sacrifice, these four warriors woke up every day looking for a way to create a better place for the next generation. Along with their teammates many of whom are with us today, took the fight up in the mountains to the east of here in Kunar. They battled like the warriors you heard of as a child. Through a storm of bullets and multiple explosions all four of these men never stopped pushing forward. The men in this Group and all other Groups would never shy from battle, they would look for the enemy and bring the fight to them. I have been doing this for nearly three decades and warfighting does not come easy. Nor does standing before you right now and paying respect to these men. They were not the only ones lost in this battle. There were many others lost in the battle from an Infantry company along with multiple injured amongst both groups of warriors. So, I ask you think of all of them as we go through this hell today and later lace up your boots, pick up your weapons and get back at it.

"Nulla victoria sine sacrificio"

LT: Team member Bourne

Bourne: When you train with your brothers for battle you become a well-oiled machine. This team is a machine that feeds off each other and Hollywood provided a lot of food for all of us. He took time to train with each member of the team individually and with each sub team to learn what made them all tick and what he needed to do to keep them all pumped up with the best training there was. I remember when we got to Kyrgyzstan, Hollywood took me aside and said "Look, we are picking up our enablers here, you go pick up their leaders and set up a meet with you Bull and me. From there we will do something to bring them into the family and let them know we are nothing without them and they are truly one with us"

This was 100% him, he did not want dissension within the family, he was transparent at all times. Never kept stuff close to his chest and was never out of the fight. Brother I will continue to live my life as you would have wanted; Team we will continue to push forward and break barriers whatever our next stop is.

To speak about Tex would be take hours. But I will bring up one memory of him that stays in my frontal lobe. It was summer about three years ago, we all were out camping together, a team weekend out. We had kayaks, coolers full of alcoholic drinks, cigars and were ready for an amazing time. We settled in Friday night and burnt some meat and drank a lot. Saturday, we get up and Tex is standing by the water butt ass naked and holding a tortilla wrapped egg sandwich in his hand. Without skipping a beat, he yells "boys, it's about time you got up, breakfast is on the table, get your shit together and let's get this party started" This was Tex all the time he gave you his all and expected nothing less from you.

I definitely will miss you Brother...

LT: Team SGT Bull

Bull stood up as Bourne came back over and gave a bro hug. He then walked slowly up to the podium. There was so much racing around his head. He could see Cali and the others in the front row, he saw all the other Green Berets from the group and other Special operators in attendance. His heart was pounding harder than any time in his life.

An eerie quiet overtakes the ceremony as Bull approaches.

Cali looks directly at him waiting on motivation.

The LT stood nervously off to the side of all the speakers.

Bull stopped and walked towards the Col and CSM gave them a handshake and a bro hug.

He then stepped in front of Chaplain Jersey and said thanks.

He turned around pointed to Cali then pointed to his chin and pushed it up, telling her to keep her head up. She smiled and gave him a thumbs up.

Bull: I am not one for the spotlight or the highlight reels. This is not something I thought I would have to do. As an NCO I did not want to have to do this. Six years ago, I was on a mission with Tex. We were attached to a different unit and were fighting in an urban environment. Our job was to clear a western alleyway of the area. Us two and two Infantry Soldiers. The first thirty minutes of the operation the plans were thrown to the side as the enemy started fighting back ferociously. The next two hours in my headset all I could hear was Tex laughing and yelling Get some! Trying to keep my composure radioing up sitreps as we cleared each area was the hardest job, I thought I would have. That day was nothing, but chaos and the operation was bogged down. We were standing back-to-back covering a corner of a building when a truck sped around a corner laying down fire on us. He pulled me back as a round crashed into my chest plate and knocked us both back. If he did not grab and pull me, it would have hit my face as I was crouched at the time. He yelled get up fucker after he dropped me on the ground. Within seconds we were moving on the truck and eliminating the threat. He saved my life that day.

We went on many missions after that, and nothing prepared me for that fight on the mountain a few days ago. Shit, the sheer number of weapons that were being fired at us throughout this battle was nuts. When Tex was hit, there truly was not a question I would get him out of there. Hollywood took control of the fight as we descended and as time went on, we could tell how desperate the fight was getting on the hill.

Hollywood showed his true character through the sequence as he fought until he physically could not anymore. He gave all he had on that hill. Doc, you did everything in your power to save him, the surgeons also gave it their best shot, however, it was just his time. He did not do anything for medals, he did it for God and country, he did it for his brothers fighting up there. He was a consummate and silent professional and we will continue his legacy in all endeavors we may pursue.

Those who did not get the chance to meet him, ask

someone and they will tell you about him, those who knew him, keep his story alive.

On that hill after long fights and multiple injuries I met two replacements. They were not strangers as they had some training with us during the past year. Jameson was a fast dude, he could beat anyone in a race, he could shoot like no one I have ever seen. When he walked up, he said we are here to fight Brother, tell me where to go and what you need, and it is done! That is a pure professional Soldier.

Puka always would laugh in training, kind of a cool mechanism to deal with craziness. He could get a person to talk in minutes of meeting them without harming them. He was a smooth and lethal character; I wish I could have operated with both of them more.

Till Valhalla Brothers!

CHAPTER 25

21 Guns

LT: Chaplain Jersey will now deliver the Benediction.

Chaplain Jersey: Please rise. Let us Pray:

Behold you oh Lord are Women and Men, Warriors in every sense of the word. They feel a sense of anger, a sense of love a sense of emptiness right now. They have walked through that shadow of the valley of death and fear no man. Fill their hearts with passion, fill their emptiness with desire a desire to complete this mission and move forward in life. We have heard stories of all four of these men. Stories of courage, of the warrior spirit, of being humble and being men of action. I sat with Tex at a meal just before they moved forward. He was a man who did not mix his words. I asked him if he wanted me to pray with him before he left, his words sent chills through me. "Padre, I love what you do for us, for our families, so don't take this the wrong way. I am a part of something bigger than me, definitely bigger than you, prayers on us will not stop a bullet from killing me or my brothers and sisters, what I need from you is to sit here and eat this meal then shake my hand and I will see you on the other side, till then go visit the hospital here and hang out with our wounded comrades" He knew it was bigger than him, as did all of them. He knew my calling should be used for all and not just him. Tex taught me more than I could ever teach him. He made me a better chaplain; he made me a better Soldier.

Our Father,

who art in heaven,

hallowed be thy name;

thy kingdom come;

thy will be done

on earth as it is in heaven.

Give us this day our daily bread;

and forgive us our trespasses

as we forgive those who trespass against us;

and lead us not into temptation,

but deliver us from evil.

For the kingdom, the power and the glory are yours now and forever.

Amen

LT: Remain standing, CSM Figtan

CSM Figtan: SFC Cali

SFC Cali: Here CSM

CSM Figtan: Technical SGT JDam

TSGT JDam: Present CSM

CSM Figtan: CPT Hollywood

Silence, three seconds pass

CSM Figtan: CPT Thomas Hollywood

Again Silence, three more seconds pass

CSM Figtan: CPT Thomas Hollywood Anderson
More Silence
CSM Figtan: SFC Tex
Silence, three seconds pass
CSM Figtan: SFC William Tex
Again Silence, three more seconds pass
CSM Figtan: SFC William Tex McGee
Silence
CSM Figtan: SSG Jameson
Silence, three seconds pass
CSM Figtan: SSG Wilson
Silence, three seconds pass
CSM Figtan: SSG Jameson Wilson
Again Silence, three more seconds pass
CSM Figtan: SSG Jameson "Irish Whiskey" Wilson
Silence, three seconds pass
CSM Figtan: SSG Martinez
Silence, three seconds pass
CSM Figtan: SSG Alberto Martinez
Again Silence, three more seconds pass
CSM Figtan: SSG Alberto "Puka Puka" Martinez
Three seconds pass
The firing squad NCO gives the command of half right face, ready, aim, fire.
The firing squad fires the first volley.
ready, aim, fire.
The second volley is fired.
Ready aim fire
The third volley is fired.

The NCO Gives the command of attention, half left face, and present arms.

Five seconds pass

A member of the band starts to play TAPS on the bugle.

CHAPTER 26

Together Alone

Bull was not doing well not being in action. Going to staff meetings and then sitting on his thumbs all day was killing him. He was bruised still and sitting idle was making his head go nuts.

Bourne, although not beat up like most of everyone else, was deep in his head as well. Not a second went by when he did not feel useless, that he did not over analyze everything going on in his head and getting antsy.

Cali had x-rays on her arm, and it was broken so she could not even escape her mind in the gym. They were all together in misery, they were together alone.

Bull gathered everyone in for a chat a week after the memorial. He asked a simple question of them all as a group.

Who wants to get out of here and reset in the States?

Doc limped up to the front of everyone and said "Bull, I have never been in a fight and felt useless before, this is the worst feeling ever, we are all injured, we are nowhere near our manning levels, logical men would say jump ship and rethink it, we are not logical men and women, we are warriors. However, as a warrior we need to recognize when we have hit our wall, and this is it, I vote for reset"

Bull: thanks Doc

Cali was up next:

"This team I led here trained for over a year for this opportunity. We are not whole right now as two of us are in Germany getting taken care of. I have a broken arm and she has 16 stitches in her head and more on her legs. When we linked up in Kyrgyzstan, I understood what our mission was and the risks. I also felt like we were part of a family. When we sat in the memorial the other day, I clinched my fists, I twitched, I was angry, just like all of you. I went for a ruck yesterday with Bull and Bourne, fuck it hurt. It hurt like no pain I ever had. It was in my heart, my head, everywhere. As much as I want to get back at it, I am seeing the signs to reset and comeback better, our brothers did not fall in vain, we did get rid of the immediate threat, the other team can handle the rest of this tour and we can come back when our number is called."

Bull asked Bourne to answer next. He stood up and said "I am the only one here who is not getting a fucking purple heart, I was stuck in ops while you fought your asses off and left it all on that hill. I listened to the radio chatter as Justice and Bull carried Tex down the hill and as Hollywood tried to keep control of the fight. I punched the radio stack no less than 12 times. You have the physical wounds to show you were here, you have invisible wounds that will not heal with a bandage or Motrin. Bull you are one of the toughest sons of bitches I have ever known and as I look at you, as I look at Doc as I look at Cali, Justice, and everyone else, I see emptiness. We need this fucking break, we need to go home, get right, get back to training and then come back to the front."

Bull stepped up next. He stood up in front of everyone with a purple Rip-It in his hand. He had drunk four already today. He took a swig and then threw the can into the wall behind him.

For some this was just theater, for Bull it was him being his true self.

"It seems like forever ago when we landed in Kyrgyzstan and met our new teammates. It seems like a lifetime ago when we started to train up for this mission. Cali, that ruck was the first one that hurt me in many years, you are not alone. This team never worked with a better enabler group than this one. JDam you and your boys are head and shoulders above any J-Tacs we have ever had. Lt Williams, your platoon was valiant and fuck I would have them on my team any day when they get healed up. Cali, when you smoked us in the lift in Kyrgyzstan, I knew we had a beast with us, when your team showed out on every workout it was solidified our team was unstoppable. During our first dual compound mission when the team was split, it was not an operator who got the first kill, it was part of our family who did. Every single one of us fought our asses off that day and every day we were at the tip of the spear. In two days, the Group Commander and an entourage will descend upon us and put medals on our chests for our actions, many of you will be receiving honors that you earned but do not want. Medals are not what we do this for, we do it for family, for the person to our left and right.

When we were stuck up on that mountain on our own with no help coming, we got shoulder to shoulder and fought, we shared ammo, we put tourniquets on, we did not care about the next hour, we cared about right fucking now. Well right fucking now we are broken, we are not doing great. It is time we all think about our futures, I know on some fucking weird plain, we should stay together and fight through this. I also have lost a lot through my career and life and do not want to lose any more. Yes, I am admitting that I feel down and out, I feel like a truck has run me over. I understand if you think less of me, it just does not make sense to keep fighting this right now. We all have mountains to climb to heal both physically and mentally. It is now we need to lead in a different fucking direction.

So long fucking story short, the day after the awards ceremony, we will depart theater, we will go and refit and make life decisions that will include either continuing in uniform or hanging up our boots. I am going to sit with my family and discuss my future. Those of you who have significant others and children, I suggest you do the same. Those of you who are single, you still have a circle of family that love you, include them in your decisions.

Cali looked up at Bull and said, "You are our leader, you will always be that being honest makes you even more of a leader than you were before, so fuck you we do not think less of you" She gave him the middle finger then a bro hug. This was followed by every member of the team doing something pretty close to the same.

After the camaraderie Bull was back to business. Tomorrow we all must go through processing and fill out paperwork to leave theater. This chapter ends in two days. What we do with the rest of our lives starts once we land in the states.

CHAPTER 27

Chest Candy

The surviving members of the team gathered at the chow hall at 0900. They all laughed, joked, and cursed at each other for 45 minutes. They also all had an entire night to think about Bull's speech the day prior. He did not miss a beat. He got pancakes, sausage and two ripits for breakfast. He sat down and was talking shit like no one's business. Cali led the team on a run and lift earlier and was laughing at her brothers now gouging themselves.

As they finished, they all looked at each other knowing the next hour or so would be ridiculous and not truly for them. The leadership usually denies awards for Soldiers based on rank as they sit behind desks in relative safety. This time all members were getting awards for Valor. Some were getting higher awards than others, but all were well deserved.

They arrived at the same location they said goodbye during the memorial a couple days before to rehearse for the awards ceremony and then receive their awards.

CSM Figtan approached the members and told them he was proud of their efforts. He then took them and was lining them up highest award to lowest. Bourne stepped to him and said stop CSM. We need to recognize all awardees as the warriors they are. There is no need to put the highest awards first to belittle the efforts of the others, they all fought until they had nothing left then gave some more. What can you say you did during their fight? CSM Figtan turned red with rage and looked at Bourne. He said listen you little shit, you do not tell me how to set up a ceremony and for fucks sake you do not weigh in on my actions during the fight. Bourne, not deterred stood firm and said "with all due respect CSM Figtan, you can take your speech and shove it, this team fought harder than any you have been on or have witnessed. Let them line up how the fuck they want, and you adjust the mother fucking delivery"!

Figtan was shocked anyone would speak to him this way. He was shocked a senior person would speak to him this way. He was angry and got into Bourne's face, was about to go ballistic on him when Col Newcomb appeared and called him over.

The entire team was laughing inside while showing professionalism on the outside. Bourne had just let the bosses know what they all believed in their hearts. Cali turned on her leadership and lined everyone up alphabetically. She knew this would fuck up the order of the ceremony, but she also believed they were all deserving, and order did not matter during this moment.

The ceremony would begin in 20 minutes and people were starting to gather at the back of the area. Col Newcomb decided to allow the formation to be as Cali made it. CSM Figtan stewed in the back of the area as no one had ever went against him like that. The team walked off and awaited orders to march up to the font of a group of people that they mostly did not know to be given awards for their actions.

They took their seats in the front row of seats to the left of the podium as looking out at the crowd. A bunch of Soldiers were arriving to the ceremony and some of the senior members who were at the memorial assembled in the seats to the direct front of the podium as they did for the service for the fallen.

CSM Figtan gave a nod to a young NCO to announce the arrival of the Officers who would be presenting the awards.

SGT Jenkins: Attention

Col Newcomb: Take your seats as he approaches the podium.

Gen Clark follows him to the speaker area along with an aide.

Col Newcomb: Good morning, a few days ago we stood here and said goodbye to amazing warriors. That was a rough day for all who we are about to talk about today. To my front left in the front two rows are the members of the same unit who were all integral to the success of the mission. Only one of the group will not be receiving a purple heart today. This team fought for what seemed like an eternity against odds that were stacked against them. These warriors sitting here in front of you fought with a tenacity not seen since Vietnam. We only could listen to their radio calls throughout the fight. In the operations center it was like watching a big game but with audio only. You want to reach out and help, but you physically cannot. I knew that this team had the best leadership around at the forefront. Even with their losses, they were strong. They kept fighting, kept digging deeper. No one on this team doubted the outcome. They looked into each other's eyes and saw intestinal fortitude that is unmatched in this world. I have been serving for 24 years now, been in countless fire fights with amazing men and women. I have always said I would never replace the teams I was a part of. However, when I heard the calmness of this team at their hour of hell, I knew they were the team we all need to strive to be on. Since I put this rank on and took command of the group, I realized I was definitely truly removed from the front, this battle made me feel alive again.

Bull, Bourne, Doc, Cali, JDam you are what leaders are. You took counter punch after counterpunch and continued to crush souls. You never thought for a minute, "I can't do this". Bourne, I know you hated being at the CoP holding it down and ensuring they had everything, but your role was equally important. Let's get this going!

CSM Figtan: Awardees Post

The team rises and marches up to the front of the crowd. Bull gives them the command of mark time then Team Halt followed by left face. They are all now facing the crowd.

LT: Attention to orders ... (he reads all the citations for each type of award)

The Team accepted their awards and were humble about it.

They then left the spotlight and prepared for a huge decision for each of them.

CHAPTER 28

Flight Home

The team processed through customs in Bagram. This is a time-honored tradition of emptying your bags for some military police or theater trained soldier to go through your stuff.

Truly feels like a check the block type activity, but the team did not care, they were about to head home.

The load up on the C17 was tedious. They were with a mix of other servicemembers leaving the country. Once the doors close and the bird lifts off, all gets quiet for a few minutes. Then an Airman announces they are out of Afghanistan airspace and the plane erupts in cheers before many of them seamlessly pass out.

After a couple hours the Airman makes another announcement, we will be landing in 20 minutes. For those who were seasoned they knew this was stop one on a long journey. Bull was sitting on a side seat and stood up to run to the latrine. He always settled into the side seats so he would not be squished in the center. Cali also got up and ran over. Bull tossed a roll of toilet paper at her as he exited the latrine and laughed. They were at ease for the first time in a while.

They find their seats again and wait for the impact of landing back in Kyrgyzstan. They feel the impact and can hear the squeal of the tires hitting the asphalt runway and slowing the big bird down.

They process into the base and are met by the Group liaison to show them to their living area. They of course had an assigned space for them and were taken care of. Most of the rest of the plane went to the three circus tents that were set up on the far side of the base. So, they were being taken care of while they waited for word of their next move.

They all set up their bunk areas in the tent then went to the shower tent. It was like a ritual when soldiers passed through Manas, get in set up clean off the theater dirt and relax. Bull went to the operations center with the roster of the entire team so they would all stay together. and be accounted for. He then went back to their tent and told them to get dressed, they are going to the morale tent for some drinks.

For conventional units they have a two-drink maximum. This did not apply to the team. They went in civilian clothes and sat in a corner to consume some cold beers and toast those they lost. They also just chatted with each other about everything they had been through. They laughed, shed some tears, and drank a lot of beers. They left the morale tent and went back to the tent. Bourne had left twenty minutes before everyone else. He was acquiring cases of beer and snacks for the tent to continue the unwinding.

When everyone got back, he had all the beer on ice and tons of junk snacks for them. The party lasted another eight hours in the hooch and they then passed out until 5 pm the next day.

Bull went to the operations center for updates on their flight out. He was told they will leave on the next bird which is expected to land in 24 hours. He went back to the hooch and provided the update to everyone. He downed a beer and then took out his burner phone and finally called home. He did not call home after the mission or even after the memorial ceremony or awards. It would not be his way, not at all.

The phone rang and it seemed like forever until Hanna answered.

Hanna: hello

Bull: Hey hot stuff

Hanna: oh, fuck what happened?

Bull: we are on our way back

Hanna: are you whole?

Bull: we are not, it was a tough one

Hanna: I Love you.

Bull: I Love You

Bull: Will call when leaving Europe

Hanna: Ok Love You Bye

Bull: Love you c u later

He then went back into the tent and sat with everyone drinking beer and relaxing. Behind the tent they had a sort of fire pit. Bull went out and lit the fire. He grabbed a six pack and told everyone the light was on. Cali came out first and they shot gunned a beer to start the night.

They did it again and drank until 7 in the morning. They set their alarms for 2 pm. The bells went off and all of them jumped up. They went to the shower tent and cleaned up, then back to the tent and secured their bags for the walk to customs again. They got in line wearing 5-11 gear and button-down shirts. The process was tedious once again. Once through they placed their bags on an air pallet that would be delivered to the bird. The team then got on a bus to the tarmac to wait for the final leg of their journey.

The bird arrives and it is a Ryan airplane. Bull always thought this was a CIA operated airline as he never seen it anywhere but in theater. They wait for the incoming personnel to get off then they load up. They care less about where they sit as long as they are near each other.

First stop is Shannon Ireland, and they get off the plane. They run to the Guinness bar and drink a few beers each then return to their seats on the plane. The next five hours over the Atlantic Ocean are quiet except for the those watching movies on their seatbacks. They arrive in the states in Baltimore. They disembark again and go through customs of their personal bags. Nothing is open except the USO in the Airport, so they go there for some snacks then back to the plane for the final leg home.

They arrive at the main base and the main team gets ready to leave the plane. Bull stops and grabs Cali and gives her a huge hug and JDam gets a big bro hug as well. They go back to their seats and wait for their final legs. Bull walks down the stairs from the plane and looks out in front of him for the van to group. They pile in and ride to the footprint. He gets out of the van, hands his weapons in to the company armorer and then gets briefed on next steps by the leaders at home.

CHAPTER 29

Reunion

Returning home after any duration of military service brings forth unique experiences. For single soldiers, the prospect of arriving to an empty home loom, leaving them to enter into solitude. On the other hand, soldiers with families are greeted with warm, enduring embraces, capturing heartwarming moments in photographs. Yet, beyond the surface of these joyful reunions, the true depth of invisible wounds begins to reveal itself once the cameras cease their clicking. These wounds can be subtle, easily dismissed with a brush-off, but others are far from subtle, profoundly affecting those in their midst and becoming nearly impossible to conceal.

In the initial week, Bull appeared to be coping well. This period involved enduring reintegration briefings and checks, with all the soldiers eagerly fixated on the goal of enjoying some time off once the week came to an end. However, the situation wasn't without its telltale signs of inner struggles. Doc, for instance, arrived each day reeking of alcohol, yet no one dared to address the issue. Justice, worn out and haggard, seemed as though sleep had eluded him throughout the entire week, yet his exhaustion went unmentioned. Bourne, on the other hand, remained on high alert, his nerves frayed, and yet no one acknowledged his apparent unease. A deafening silence surrounded these individuals, their unspoken burdens hanging in the air.

Despite the dismissive atmosphere surrounding their outward struggles, Bull's internal battle raged on relentlessly. Though he mechanically went through the motions of displaying affection towards his family and fulfilling his duties during the week, his inner turmoil was undeniable. Deep down, Bull was acutely aware of his own emotional and psychological disarray, but he also understood the consequences of admitting his struggles at this moment. To disclose any issues would undoubtedly lead the group to cast him aside, potentially relegating him to administrative tasks or worse. Faced with this grim prospect, Bull made a conscious decision to bury his pain deep within, allowing it to fester silently, unseen by others.

The week of reintegration finally came to an end, signaling the beginning of a two-week leave for the soldiers. Before parting ways, they gathered at a local bar, indulging in drinks until the early morning hours. It was Friday night, and the absence of battle-induced adrenaline left them feeling drained. The road ahead was uncertain, and for the first time, they all confronted the vastness of the unknown.

Bull, sensing his own exhaustion, reached out to Hanna, requesting a ride at the ungodly hour of 4 a.m. Hanna, concerned for his well-being, insisted on arranging an Uber for him. In addition, Bull took a moment to check in with Cali, hoping she was doing alright. However, an immediate response eluded him.

They stumbled out of the bar, fatigue and alcohol weighing them down. On the sidewalk, Doc succumbed to his excessive indulgence, vomiting unceremoniously, eliciting laughter from the group. Amidst the shared camaraderie, they jumped into the Rav-4 Uber and embarked on their journey home. As the Uber driver maneuvered through the familiar streets, making stops at each soldier's house, they bid farewell with bro hugs and promises to meet again soon. Bull, the last to be dropped off, expressed his gratitude to the driver, thanking him for the ride and telling him to be safe out there.

CHAPTER 30

Chaos

The following day, Bull awoke disoriented, finding himself in his own garage. His knuckles were scraped and raw, as though he had engaged in a night-long bout of bare-knuckle boxing. Confusion and concern washed over him as he surveyed the scene. His heavy bag was splattered with blood, scattered weights littered the garage floor. Dressed only in boxer shorts, his head throbbing with a relentless headache, he glanced at the clock—it read 1 PM.

Summoning his strength, Bull rose from the floor and cleared away the remnants of his chaotic outburst, tidying up the weight debris. He located his jeans and slipped them on, mustering the energy to climb the stairs from the garage into the house. As he stepped inside, an eerie silence enveloped him. Time verification became essential—his watch, his phone, and finally the microwave confirmed the hour.

In a desperate attempt to make contact, Bull called out Hanna's name, but there was no response, only the empty echo of his own voice. He glanced upon the kitchen island, and his eyes fell upon a note that had been left behind. With a tremor in his voice, he read the words aloud: "Hey, you had a bit of a breakdown in the garage. I've taken Shelly, and we're spending the day at a hotel to give you some space. We love you, and we'll see you tomorrow."

Overwhelmed, Bull staggered backward, his body finding solace in a nearby chair beside the island. He slumped into it, burying his face in his hands, and then unleashed a scream of raw frustration and disbelief, venting the weight of his anguish with a resounding, "What the fuck?!"

Meanwhile, a mile away from Bull's garage, Doc gradually regained consciousness, his surroundings registering as he felt the grass beneath him. The self-medication he had been relying on since their departure from Afghanistan had taken its toll. Upon exiting the Uber, he had instinctively sought solace in alcohol, grabbing another bottle of Jameson before stumbling out onto the back deck.

Doc harbored a deep secret that he had concealed from the team throughout their deployment—his wife had left him months ago, and they were now in the midst of a painful divorce. Either his comrades failed to notice the changes in him or deliberately avoided addressing the matter. Pushing himself up from the ground, Doc realized he was barefoot, though otherwise clothed. His gaze fell upon the two empty bottles on the deck, a stark reminder of his ongoing struggle.

He shuffled back inside, heading straight for his bedroom, seeking refuge in the familiar space. Without hesitation, he stepped into the shower, allowing the water to cascade over him. In that moment, he stood, fixated on the showerhead, his mind racing with a torrent of thoughts. Doc acknowledged the troubling state of his mental well-being, despising the turmoil that consumed him, aware that he was far from a healthy headspace.

Across town, in the bustling city center, Justice slowly stirred from his uneasy slumber, finding himself sprawled on a cold concrete bench. His torn t-shirt bore the remnants of dried blood, mirroring the state of his khaki 5-11 pants, which were also ripped and stained with dirt and blood. Clad in orange flip-flops, the only possession provided to him by the guards, he found himself surrounded by four or five other individuals who had also spent the night in the holding cell.

With no clock in sight and stripped of personal belongings, determining the time proved challenging for Justice. As he tried to collect his bearings, a guard approached, greeting him with a casual "welcome back, sleepy. How do you feel?" The question hung in the air, demanding Justice to confront the physical and emotional toll of his recent experiences.

Curious about the duration of his stay, Justice inquired with the guard, asking how long he had been confined in the holding cell. The guard informed him that it was currently 4:30 PM and, according to the previous shift, Justice had been brought in at 5 in the morning. The realization of spending over eleven hours in the cell weighed heavily on his throbbing head and aching ribs.

Seeking clarity regarding the reason for his detainment, Justice turned to the guard once more, voicing his confusion. The guard replied that his attorney would provide the necessary information once they arrived. Justice asked if he could make a phone call. The guard assured him that after completing the rounds, he would assist Justice in getting his turn to make a phone call. A glimmer of hope emerged, offering a chance to reach out and gain some clarity amidst the confusion and uncertainty surrounding his situation.

Upon Bourne's arrival home, his wife enveloped him in a tight embrace, her warmth and care providing a sense of comfort. She questioned whether he had managed to release whatever was troubling him, emphasizing the importance of finding solace. Knowing he was in good hands, Bourne allowed himself to be guided to bed, surrendering to the fatigue that had settled upon him.

The following day at noon, his wife returned, rousing him from his slumber. Bourne, refreshed from his rest, promptly took a shower, and dressed himself. Together, they embarked on a journey to the airport, bound for the serene shores of Hawaii, where they could unwind and find respite from the weight of their world.

As they settled into their seats on the airplane, Bourne turned to his wife, expressing his love for her. With a sense of hope and anticipation, he voiced his wishes for his buddies, hoping that they had experienced an equally rejuvenating night and morning. As the plane gathered momentum on the runway, ready for takeoff towards the distant island paradise, Bourne's thoughts lingered on the well-being of his fellow soldiers, carrying a glimmer of optimism for their collective journey ahead.

CHAPTER 31

Justice

Led by the guard, Justice was escorted to a phone, his only connection to the outside world. With a flicker of hope, he dialed the numbers, attempting to reach out to his comrades Bull, Doc, and Bourne. Unfortunately, there was no answer on any of their ends, leaving him without the support he sought in that moment. Determined to secure his release, Justice instead reached out to his father, who resided 2000 miles away, explaining his predicament and seeking assistance.

After concluding the call, Justice's attention was drawn back to the guard, who informed him that his attorney had arrived. Guided to a separate room, he was met by a public defender, ready to shed light on the charges leveled against him. As the conversation unfolded, Justice was presented with fragments of the narrative, piecing together how he had transitioned from the confines of the Rav-4 to the confines of the jail cell. The attorney aimed to provide clarity, unraveling the events that led to Justice's current predicament and discussing potential legal avenues moving forward.

As the weight of the charges pressed upon him, Justice's head drooped, and his broad shoulders slumped under the burden. With a mixture of disbelief and a growing sense of remorse, he inquired about the individuals he was accused of assaulting. Pamela, his court-appointed attorney, began to recount the events that transpired.

According to Pamela, the incident unfolded when Justice encountered difficulty using his house key to gain entry, leading him to create a disturbance. In response, his neighbors, Mike, Nancy, and their son Jeremy, emerged from their home to help. However, tensions escalated rapidly. Witnesses, including Mike, reported that Justice unleashed a torrent of verbal abuse towards them, ultimately shoving Jeremy to the ground. Reacting to the assault on his son, Mike lunged at Justice, resulting in a violent altercation wherein Justice unleashed a barrage of fists and kicks upon him. Jeremy, attempting to protect his father, also found himself subjected to the same onslaught.

Amidst the chaos, Nancy, realizing the severity of the situation, contacted the police and rushed outside in an attempt to intervene. However, Justice seized her hand and, with alarming force, flipped her over his shoulder, causing her to collide with the fence that was between their properties. In the aftermath of this encounter, Nancy lay motionless, employing her stillness as a desperate measure to keep Justice at bay.

The gravity of the situation sank in for Justice as the details unfolded, painting a picture of a violent and disturbing incident involving his neighbors. A profound sense of remorse washed over him, accompanied by the realization that his actions had caused harm and had legal consequences.

As the chaos unfolded, the police swiftly responded to Nancy's distress call, arriving at the scene within minutes. However, instead of cooperating, Justice defiantly confronted the officers, shouting for everyone to seek cover and urging them to control their fire. Tensions escalated further as he lunged at the nearest officer, prompting the other law enforcement personnel to scan the surroundings, assessing the situation for any additional threats.

A tumultuous five-minute struggle ensued, with Justice fiercely resisting arrest. In an attempt to subdue him, the officers resorted to using a Taser, eventually rendering him motionless and facilitating his transportation to the local jail. Meanwhile, an ambulance arrived to tend to the injured parties, including an unconscious Mike, a battered Jeremy, and a distraught Nancy.

Pamela, his court-appointed attorney, informed Justice that bail would not be granted until his appearance before the Judge, scheduled for Monday. Additionally, she relayed the message that his unit had been notified and awaited his release to speak with him, indicating that his military leadership was concerned about his well-being and eager to provide support. The weight of the situation bore down on Justice, as he grappled with the consequences of his actions and the impending legal proceedings that lay ahead.

CHAPTER 32

Doc

Despite the countless deployments and harrowing fire-fights, he had experienced throughout his years of service, Doc had never felt as lost and burdened as he did now. This time was different. Just before the deployment, his marriage had crumbled, leaving him to return home to an empty house and a sense of overwhelming responsibility resting squarely on his shoulders.

The weight of these circumstances seemed insurmountable, and Doc struggled to find a way out of the chaos that plagued his mind. The darkness within him deepened with each passing day, enveloping his thoughts and emotions. The combination of the traumatic experiences abroad and the personal turmoil he faced at home created a profound sense of despair, leaving him grasping for a glimmer of hope. It was a daunting battle, one that Doc had yet to conquer, and he found himself navigating uncharted territory, unsure of how to emerge from the depths of his own darkness.

Doc, seeking solace and temporary respite from his inner turmoil, turned to his familiar refuge – the liquor cabinet. Retrieving a bottle of Jameson, he also gathered a jar of filthy cherries and a bottle of ginger ale. With deliberate movements, he filled his favorite glass with ice, a vessel that had witnessed many similar moments.

Pouring the amber liquid into the glass, Doc embarked on another day of numbing the pain through self-medication. The alcohol served as a temporary escape, providing a fleeting sense of relief from the weight of his emotional burdens. In this repetitive ritual, he sought solace in the numbing embrace of intoxication, albeit knowing deep down that it was a temporary fix, incapable of truly healing the wounds within.

As he took a sip, the familiar burn and the slight sweetness mingled on his tongue, momentarily easing the ache that gnawed at his soul. For now, it was a fleeting moment of reprieve, a brief respite from the darkness that consumed him.

CHAPTER 33

Bull

As Bull glanced at his phone, the missed call from the county jail caught his attention. Initially dismissing it as a mistake or a wrong number, he overlooked its significance. However, as he scrolled through his messages, he discovered Cali's response from earlier in the day. Her struggle with reintegration weighed heavily on her, and Bull felt compelled to offer his support, assuring her that he was there if she needed someone to talk to.

Seeking camaraderie and a sense of normalcy, Bull attempted to reach out to his brothers. First, he dialed Justice's number, hoping to share a laugh about the events of the previous night. Yet, there was no answer. Undeterred, he tried contacting Bourne, but knowing he had departed for vacation, Bull's expectations were low. The disappointment continued when Doc failed to pick up as well. Left with an overwhelming sense of loneliness, Bull found himself alone in his house, devoid of someone to vent to or share his thoughts with.

Overwhelmed by this new territory of isolation and struggling to cope, Bull turned to drinking as a means to dull his emotions and numb the pain. Unfamiliar with navigating this kind of emotional landscape, he sought solace in alcohol, hoping to find temporary relief from the overwhelming weight of his circumstances.

CHAPTER 34

Pieces

Two weeks had passed, and the team reconvened at the Team Room, signaling the end of their break. Bull, the first to arrive, appeared far from refreshed, having already visited the gym before changing into his work clothes. He patiently waited for the rest of the team to join him. At 8:30, Bourne entered the room, radiating a sun-kissed glow and exuding a sense of rejuvenation. They exchanged greetings and caught up on the events of the past two weeks, but both expressed their concern over the silence from Justice and Doc, having received no communication from either of them.

Just as their conversation reached its peak, Captain DP Hardsell made his entrance, commanding their attention. He requested that they take a seat, and Bull and Bourne settled onto the couch, bracing themselves for what was to come. Hardsell proceeded to deliver a briefing, revealing the troubling news of Justice's incarceration. The gravity of the situation hit Bull like a jolt, and he sprang up from his seat, demanding to know when this had occurred and why they had only just learned of it.

Hardsell informed them that Justice's arrest had taken place early on the Saturday that marked the beginning of their leave, leaving Bull and Bourne stunned by the delayed notification. The abrupt revelation cast a cloud of uncertainty and concern over the team, as they grappled with the knowledge that one of their own was facing serious charges, with a future that appeared grim.

Bourne's concern deepened as he leaned forward, echoing Bull's sentiment and questioning why they were only being informed now. The explanation given by Hardsell, regarding the rear detachment command's decision to handle matters without involving them, did little to appease their frustration. Bull's anger erupted as he vehemently expressed his discontent, emphasizing the importance of their tight-knit bond as a family and denouncing the excuse given.

Attempting to restore order, Hardsell urged Bull to gather himself, reminding him that there was more information to be shared. The tension in the room remained palpable as Bourne braced himself, his mind consumed with worry for Doc, who was notably absent at that moment.

Hardsell proceeded with the next piece of news, delivering it with a heavy tone. He revealed that just the previous night, emergency medical personnel and the police had been dispatched to Doc's residence in response to a welfare check. Concerned by his ex-wife's unsuccessful attempts to reach him, along with the worry expressed by his family, authorities were called for assistance. Upon arriving at Doc's house, they discovered him unconscious, lying face down on the bedroom floor, wearing only his socks. The room was littered with multiple bottles of liquor and a bottle of pills. Doc was currently in the intensive care unit at the base hospital, relying on a ventilator to support his breathing. Hardsell somberly acknowledged that if he were to recover, the road ahead would be arduous and lengthy.

The weight of the news settled heavily on the team, amplifying their collective sense of shock and concern. The stark reality of the situations involving both Justice and Doc created an atmosphere of uncertainty and fear, as they grappled with the repercussions of their brother's respective challenges.

Bourne absorbed the weight of the news regarding Doc's condition, he shifted his attention back to Captain Hardsell, his eyes filled with a mix of frustration and resignation. With a touch of bitterness, he asked the captain if there was any further news to be shared. Hardsell, with a solemn expression, informed Bourne that he had been assigned as the new team leader, though he wished it could have been under better circumstances.

Bourne's exclamation of frustration captured the sentiment of the moment, expressing his disappointment in the circumstances that had led to Hardsell's new role on the team. "Well, fuck," he uttered, reflecting the weight of the responsibility that now fell upon the young Captain's shoulders. Despite the heavy atmosphere, he mustered a glimmer of determination, acknowledging that there was much work to be done moving forward.

In a gesture of solidarity, Bull leaned towards Hardsell, offering a handshake as a sign of support and partnership. However, he couldn't resist adding a hint of criticism, urging

Hardsell to work on the delivery of news. With that, Bull walked away, his mind focused on finding a way to navigate the challenging circumstances that had befallen the team.

The weight of the situations involving Justice and Doc, along with the team's new dynamics, weighed heavily on Hardsell as he prepared to take on his new role. It was a daunting journey ahead, with many obstacles to overcome, and the team now faced the task of rallying together to navigate the troubled waters that lay before them.

Against the orders from those in positions of authority, the team made their way to the hospital, driven by an unwavering determination to be there for Doc, their comrade who had been by their side during challenging times. However, the hospital staff denied them access to the ICU, leaving them only with a brief update on Doc's deteriorating condition. The news they received painted a grim picture, leaving them disheartened and filled with a sense of helplessness.

They retreated to the hospital parking lot, the weight of their individual struggles and emotions became apparent. Bourne, in a moment of compassion, turned to Bull, asking him how he was holding up. Bull, his voice heavy with pain, shared the deep-seated turmoil that had plagued him. Hanna, unable to stay at their home with him or leave him alone with their daughter, had sought refuge with friends across town for safety. Bull confessed to the raging battles he fought within himself, unleashing his frustrations on the heavy bag, lifting weights, and drowning his sorrows in alcohol. A wave of regret washed over him as he recalled the missed call from the jail that Saturday, cursing himself for letting Justice down.

Bourne empathized, revealing that he, too, had missed a

call during his flight to Hawaii, only remembering it now in the midst of their current situation. He shared that he had felt rejuvenated after their vacation until this very moment. The weight of the circumstances they faced weighed heavily upon them, and Bourne acknowledged the difficult reality of the day. In this moment, the bond between Bull and Bourne grew stronger as they found solace in their shared struggles and acknowledged the challenges that lay before them.

CRUSHED

The complexities of Bull's home front have become increasingly overwhelming. As he fights to salvage his marriage, the anger and rage issues that have plagued him present significant challenges. Moreover, the connection he forged with Cali during their text exchanges before the leave has added fuel to the fire of his marital problems. The situation took a turn for the worse when, unbeknownst to Bull, Hanna saw a text from Cali on his phone. The misinterpretation immediately ignited a heated argument between them.

Despite Bull's attempts to explain that their connection was borne out of shared experiences during their time together in Afghanistan and that it was merely a means of checking on each other, Hanna's emotions were too raw to be appeased. In the heat of the moment, she stormed out of the house, taking their daughter Shelly with her, leaving Bull feeling even more isolated and trapped in the darkness that had enveloped him.

With his emotions in turmoil, Bull sought solace in the familiar refuge of alcohol and the heavy bag. The drinking intensified, serving as a temporary escape from the emotional turmoil he faced. The relentless pounding on the bag became a physical manifestation of the internal battles he waged within himself.

As the days passed, Bull found himself caught in a vicious cycle, unable to escape the depths of his despair. The conflicts both abroad and at home had taken a significant toll, leaving him grappling with the weight of his emotions and the challenges that lay ahead. In this difficult moment, Bull's support system felt fragmented, with Hanna and Cali representing conflicting aspects of his life. The path forward seemed uncertain, and he found himself navigating a dark and tumultuous journey with no clear resolution in sight.

Hanna's heartache was palpable as she grappled with the difficult decision she had to make. Despite the challenges in their marriage and Bull's struggle with anger and rage, she couldn't bring herself to give up on their love. Deep down, she knew that for their relationship to stand a chance, Bull needed to address his issues and work on himself. She longed for the man she first met, the one she fell in love with, and desperately hoped he could find his way back to that version of himself.

Seeing the pain in Shelly's innocent questions about when they could return home to see her dad and play with her toys was an additional weight on Hanna's heart. She understood the impact this separation had on their daughter, and it pained her to witness the toll it took on their family. Yet, Hanna remained steadfast in her conviction that it was essential for Bull to face his demons and make positive changes for their family's future.

It was a difficult journey for Hanna, torn between her love for Bull and the need for him to confront his issues before they could truly rebuild their life together. As much as it hurt, she knew that prioritizing Bull's personal growth was necessary for the well-being of their relationship and the happiness of their daughter. In her heart, she held on to hope that, with time and effort, they could find their way back to one another, stronger and more resilient than before.

CHAPTER 35

Hits Keep Coming

The weight of the past month's events bore down heavily on Bull, Bourne, Doc, and Justice, leaving them all feeling emotionally and physically drained. Doc's condition remained unchanged, leaving the medical staff grappling with the difficult task of finding a solution to bring him back from the brink.

Justice's court hearing had not offered any relief either, as his charges were elevated to attempted murder, accompanied by the weight of attempted manslaughter charges for the harm inflicted on Jeremy and Nancy. The aftermath of Justice's actions had left the neighbors physically and emotionally scarred, with Jeremy still dealing with the consequences of his injuries and Nancy undergoing therapy to aid her healing process.

As for Bull, the turbulence in his personal life and the devastation he witnessed among his comrades weighed heavily on his soul. He felt an overwhelming sense of helplessness, experiencing emotions he had never encountered before in his career. The loss of Hanna and Shelly, coupled with the dire situation of Doc and Justice, left him adrift in a sea of darkness. Faced with an insurmountable burden, he found himself making choices that only further deepened his descent into despair.

In the face of such overwhelming challenges, Bull was at risk of losing himself to the darkness that consumed him. The road ahead seemed bleak and uncertain, with no clear path to healing or redemption. It was a critical juncture for all of them, one that would require tremendous strength, resilience, and support to find a way out of the abyss that threatened to swallow them whole.

HELP!!!!!!

Bourne's journey to find his center and address his inner turmoil had been a revelation for him. He recognized the need for change and had taken significant steps to better himself, seeking help through counseling, reducing his drinking, and embracing meditation to find peace within. The moment he looked at himself in the mirror and saw the anger and lost soul staring back, he knew he had to act.

His wife had been a source of unwavering support, understanding the importance of him having one last night with his comrades before fully embarking on his path of self-discovery. Her thoughtful gesture of booking a trip to Hawaii, focused on rejuvenation, self-reflection, and meditation, touched Bourne deeply. It was a surprise that exceeded his expectations, and he gratefully accepted her love and support. As the days turned into weeks, Bourne continued to focus on his personal growth, becoming more attuned to his own well-being. However, amidst his journey, he unintentionally overlooked the struggles his brothers were facing. The circumstances surrounding Bull, Doc, and Justice weighed heavily on them, each facing their own battles with no easy solutions in sight.

Bourne realized that while he was making progress and finding his way, his brothers were still lost in the depths of their own challenges. As he looked around, he realized that he could only save one person in this situation - himself. It was a harsh reality to confront, but he knew that he could not force others to change or heal. All he could do was be there for them if they sought help, just as his wife had been there for him.

Bourne's journey was not only about his personal growth but also about recognizing the limitations of his influence and learning to let go when necessary. He would continue to support his brothers and be there for them if they needed it, but he understood that their paths to healing were their own to navigate. In this moment of realization, he found a deeper sense of compassion and empathy, knowing that everyone's journey to recovery was unique, and he could only control his own.

Bourne felt a newfound sense of purpose, having realized the transformative power of seeking help and working on his own mental well-being. He understood the gravity of mental health and its impact on a warrior's effectiveness, both on the battlefield and at home. Recognizing the danger of a loose cannon, he now felt determined to help his friend, Bull, find his way back from the darkness and into a life worth living.

Armed with the knowledge he gained during his own journey to wellness, Bourne researched various avenues to assist Bull in seeking help and finding clarity. He understood that convincing Bull to see the same picture he now saw might be an uphill battle. Bull had endured tremendous loss and was struggling immensely, making it challenging for him to see a way out of his current state.

Bourne knew the road ahead would be difficult, as Bull had lost everything, he held dear. Convincing him to make a 180-degree turn towards getting better would require patience, empathy, and understanding. He realized that it might be hard for Bull to see a way forward in his current state of despair.

Nevertheless, Bourne was committed to being there for

his friend and to help him navigate the path to recovery. He hoped that his own journey to wellness and transformation could serve as an inspiration for Bull, showing him that change was possible, even in the darkest times. Bourne understood that he couldn't force Bull to accept help, but he would be a steadfast support, patiently offering guidance and encouragement when the time was right.

Bourne's mission was to be there for his friend, to help him see that there was still hope and a chance for healing. He would do everything in his power to convince Bull that seeking help and finding the strength to face his demons was not a sign of weakness but rather an act of courage. He knew that the road ahead would be challenging, but Bourne was determined to do whatever it took to help Bull find his way back to living, not just existing.

HELL NO

The weight of the news hit Bourne like a sledgehammer to the chest. He had braced himself for the possibility of losing Doc, given his critical condition, but he never expected to hear that Justice had taken his own life. The shock and grief flooded over him, leaving him speechless for a moment.

Bourne had built a strong connection with Justice during their time together, and the news of his friend's passing was devastating. He thought about how Justice had struggled since returning home, burdened by the invisible wounds of war. The pain in his heart was matched only by the sorrow he knew Justice's family would endure.

Captain Hardsell's words cut through the silence, conveying the sadness that now engulfed the team. He informed Bourne that the command and Justice's family had been notified, leaving no doubt that the reality of this tragedy was unfolding. The grief was overwhelming, and Bourne felt the weight of responsibility as he wondered if there was more, he could have done to help Justice.

Bourne's mind raced with memories of their time together, the laughter, the camaraderie, and the shared hardships. He thought about Justice's struggles, wishing he had found a way to reach out and help his friend in those dark moments. He couldn't help but feel an overwhelming sense of loss and guilt.

As the news settled in, Bourne knew that he now faced an even greater challenge in helping Bull. The pain of losing one of their own was a stark reminder of the battles they all fought, both on and off the battlefield. He resolved to honor

Justice's memory by doing everything in his power to help Bull find his way back from the darkness. The loss of their brother would serve as a haunting reminder of the importance of reaching out for help and standing united as a family, no matter the struggles they faced.

In the face of tragedy, Bourne knew he couldn't give up on Bull, even if the task ahead seemed daunting. He would do everything he could to be there for his friend, to offer support, and to remind him that he was not alone in his pain. Together, they would find a way to honor Justice's memory and support each other through the darkness that now surrounded them.

The news of Justice's passing had shaken Bull to his core. Bourne's powerful words and the reality of losing a brother in arms snapped him out of the haze of self-pity and despair. The weight of the loss reminded him of the responsibility he had as a leader and as a member of their close-knit unit. Bull realized that he had neglected his duty to support his comrades, and his eyes were finally opened to the magnitude of the situation.

Bourne knew that they needed to come together as a team and support one another during this incredibly difficult time. He saw a spark of determination in Bull's eyes as he expressed the need to find himself and restore what he could. The loss of Justice and the realization of losing Hanna pushed him to a turning point.

With the memorial for Justice planned for the next week, Bourne and Bull now had a purpose to focus on. They would honor their fallen brother with a heartfelt eulogy, sharing stories of his bravery and accomplishments in combat. It was a way to keep Justice's memory alive and celebrate the life he lived.

Despite the grief and shock, Bourne and Bull also felt the need to visit Doc, even if he was incoherent. However, when they arrived at the hospital, they received another devastating blow - Doc had also passed away, leaving them heartbroken and in disbelief. Bull's emotional dam burst, and he broke down in tears, unable to contain the overwhelming pain of losing two dear friends.

Bourne did his best to support Bull, pulling him close and carrying the weight of their collective grief. He called Captain Hardsell to share the devastating news, knowing that the memorial they planned would now be for two fallen brothers.

In this moment of sorrow, Bourne and Bull realized the importance of being there for one another, no matter the challenges they faced. They knew they had to hold on to the memories of their fallen friends and honor their legacies by supporting each other through the darkness. In the face of loss, they understood that they could not let grief consume them, but instead, they had to find strength in their bond as a unit, as brothers and sisters who had shared the burdens of war together.

TRIANGLE OF STARS

Bourne stood up, gave Bull a solemn nod, and stepped to the podium. His heart was heavy, and his mind was filled with memories of the fallen brothers. As he looked out at the crowd, he saw the faces of their friends, families, and fellow soldiers, all gathered to pay their respects to Justice and Doc.

He began his eulogy with a deep breath, trying to steady his emotions. He spoke of Justice's unwavering determination and loyalty, his courage under fire, and his selflessness in putting others before himself. He recounted the countless times Justice had stepped up to protect his fellow soldiers and the incredible impact he had on everyone around him.

Then, Bourne shifted his focus to Doc. He spoke of his compassion and kindness, how he cared for the wounded with unwavering dedication, and how he always put others' needs above his own. He shared stories of Doc's calming presence, a reassuring figure in the midst of chaos, and the many lives he had saved on the battlefield.

Bourne's voice quivered as he spoke about the struggles both Justice and Doc faced when they returned home. He acknowledged that the transition from the battlefield to civilian life was not easy for any of them. He emphasized the importance of supporting one another, of being there for each other, even when it seemed like the world was against them.

With tears in his eyes, Bourne urged everyone in the room to honor Justice and Doc's memory by taking care of each other. He emphasized that their legacy would live on through the bonds they had forged and the impact they had on their brothers and sisters in arms. As he concluded his eulogy, Bourne thanked the crowd for being there to remember and celebrate the lives of their fallen comrades. He reminded them that they were not alone in their grief and that they had each other to lean on during the darkest of times.

Bull stood next to Bourne, listening to his words, and feeling the weight of the loss they had endured. He couldn't help but think about the journey they had ahead of them, healing together and supporting one another through the pain. As Bull delivered his eulogy, the weight of their loss and the impact of their struggles reverberated through the room. He spoke from the heart, honoring the bravery and sacrifice of Justice and Doc on the battlefield. He reminded everyone of the immense courage and selflessness they had shown in the face of danger, saving their fellow soldiers, and giving everything for the sake of others.

However, Bull also made it clear that after their deployment, they had not received the support they needed. The battles they faced off the battlefield were just as real and challenging as the ones they encountered on foreign soil. He acknowledged that they, as a unit, had failed each other during this time of darkness and despair.

In a powerful moment of raw honesty, Bull addressed the leaders in the room. He called them out for their lack of awareness and understanding of what their warriors were going through. He demanded that they step up and take responsibility for the well-being of their soldiers, to see beyond the PowerPoint presentations and connect with their people on a human level.

Bull's own struggle with rage, anger, and the breakdown

of his marriage served as a stark example of the toll that war and its aftermath can take on a soldier's life. He emphasized the need for support, understanding, and genuine care from leadership and fellow soldiers alike. The call for better mental health care and proactive support for those struggling became the driving force behind his words.

In a brave and heart-wrenching admission, Bull declared that he was not the warrior he once was. He recognized the toll the events had taken on him and expressed his intention to focus on rebuilding his life and supporting his brothers and sisters who faced similar challenges upon returning home.

His eulogy was a call to action, a plea for change and an end to the suffering of those who serve. As he handed over the podium to the Chaplain, the silence in the room was palpable, and the impact of his words resonated deeply with everyone present.

With Bull's powerful message ringing in their ears, the attendees of the memorial were left to reflect on the sacrifices made by Justice and Doc and the urgent need for better support systems for returning soldiers. Their legacy would be more than their bravery on the battlefield; it would be the catalyst for change in the way their brothers and sisters were cared for beyond the frontlines.

The memorial service ended with a solemn farewell to Justice and Doc, the two fallen warriors who had given their all-in service to their country. The chapel was filled with a sense of unity and determination as the attendees left, vowing to never forget the sacrifices made and the bonds forged in the crucible of war.

In the weeks and months that followed, Bourne and Bull,

along with their fellow soldiers, took the lessons learned from their fallen brothers to heart. They worked together to create a support system within their unit, ensuring that no one would feel alone or abandoned in their struggles.

Their journey towards healing was far from easy, but they knew that they had to honor the memory of Justice and Doc by taking care of each other. They had to be the family they needed in times of darkness, just as their fallen comrades had been for them in the past. And as they faced the challenges of life after war, Bourne and Bull found solace in knowing that they had each other, and they had the memory of their fallen brothers to guide them through the darkest days. They were forever bound by the bonds of brotherhood, and they vowed to carry on the legacy of Justice and Doc for the rest of their lives.

NEW BEGINNINGS

Bourne's decision to stay in and work alongside Captain Hardsell marked a new chapter in his military career. Determined to make a positive change, he recognized that rebuilding the team from scratch was an opportunity to create an environment where soldiers could receive the support and care they needed.

Together, Bourne and Hardsell worked tirelessly to implement new protocols and initiatives aimed at improving mental health support for their soldiers. They collaborated with mental health professionals, therapists, and counselors to develop comprehensive programs to address the unique challenges faced by those returning from combat.

The focus shifted from just training for the battlefield to preparing soldiers for life beyond their service. Bourne and Hardsell knew that developing resilient and mentally strong warriors would ultimately lead to stronger bonds within the team and fewer cases of struggling soldiers left to suffer in silence.

The new team became a safe space for soldiers to express their feelings and share their experiences without judgment. Bourne openly shared his own journey towards healing, encouraging others to seek help when needed. He became a mentor and support system for his fellow soldiers, offering guidance and understanding in times of difficulty.

With Bull's support, Bourne also reached out to those who had left the military and were transitioning into civilian life. He realized that support shouldn't end at the base gate; it should extend to veterans as they navigated the challenges of adjusting to civilian society.

The efforts of Bourne and Captain Hardsell did not go unnoticed. The leadership recognized their dedication to the well-being of their soldiers, and their model was adopted by other units across the military. The impact of their work spread beyond their base, influencing the approach to mental health care throughout the armed forces.

As they continued their mission, they always kept the memory of Justice and Doc close to their hearts. They knew that their fallen brothers' sacrifice had sparked a powerful change within them, motivating them to be better leaders and advocates for their soldiers.

Through their resilience, dedication, and unwavering commitment, Bourne and Hardsell proved that the true measure of a warrior's strength goes beyond the battlefield. They showed that caring for each other and fostering a supportive environment could be just as crucial in ensuring the success and well-being of the team.

Bourne stood by Bull's side throughout the counseling process, providing unwavering support and encouragement. As Bull confronted his inner demons, he began to find some solace in the therapy sessions. Opening up about his experiences in combat and the struggles he faced at home allowed him to start healing.

The counseling sessions also gave Bull the tools he needed to address his anger and rage in healthier ways. He learned coping mechanisms and techniques to manage his emotions, allowing him to break free from the cycle of self-destructive behavior.

Throughout the process, Bourne remained a steadfast friend, always ready to lend an ear and offer guidance. He shared his own experiences of seeking help and encouraged Bull to take it one step at a time, reminding him that healing was a journey that required patience and self-compassion.

Despite the divorce, Hanna understood the importance of Bull's journey to healing. She cared for him deeply but knew that they both needed space to find their own paths forward. She was proud of Bull for seeking help and taking responsibility for his actions. Though their marriage had come to an end, she hoped that both of them could eventually find peace and happiness in their separate ways.

As the months passed, Bull's transformation was evident to those around him. He was no longer the same man consumed by anger and pain. Instead, he was determined to be a better version of himself, someone who could carry the memories of his fallen brothers with honor and strength.

Bourne continued to work closely with Bull, providing a support system as he navigated life after the military. Together, they focused on building a community of veterans who could lean on each other during difficult times. They attended support groups, organized events, and shared their experiences to help others find their way to healing. As they moved forward, Bull found a new purpose in helping his fellow veterans. He became an advocate for mental health support within the military and worked to raise awareness about the challenges veterans face upon returning home. His own journey of healing became a source of inspiration for others, showing them that seeking help was a sign of strength, not weakness.

Bull's move to California brought him back into Cali's life

in a significant way. Both having left the military; they found solace in each other's company and formed a deep bond born from shared experiences and a desire to make a difference in the lives of veterans.

Together, they founded an organization focused on providing mental health support and resources to veterans struggling with the aftermath of their service. Drawing from their own journeys of healing and transformation, they knew the importance of offering a safe and understanding space for veterans to seek help.

Their organization offered counseling services, support groups, and workshops tailored to address the unique challenges veterans faced. They brought in experts from various fields to provide comprehensive care, including trauma-informed therapy, mindfulness practices, and other evidence-based approaches to healing.

As they worked tirelessly to build their organization, Bull and Cali's partnership grew stronger. They were not only life partners but also partners in their mission to help those who had served their country. Their shared experiences brought a profound understanding of the struggles veterans faced, enabling them to connect with those seeking support on a deeper level.

Their dedication and passion for their cause earned them respect and admiration within the veteran community. Word spread about their organization, and more veterans sought their help. Bull and Cali's tireless efforts in raising awareness about mental health within the military earned them recognition from various organizations and institutions.

Their journey was not without challenges, but they faced

them together, bolstered by their love for one another and their shared mission. The memory of Doc and Justice served as a constant reminder of the urgency and importance of their work. Bull and Cali knew that every life they touched could make a difference in someone's battle with mental health issues.

MOVING FORWARD

While this is the end of service in uniform for Bull and Cali, they have moved forward with their new organization. The lights are not off with the Team as Bourne and Hardsell will continue to build the new team and continue their journey of service. Keep on pushing forward and they will greet you with their next mission soon.

Printed in the USA
CPSIA information can be obtained
at www.ICGtesting.com
LVHW021652111023
760672LV00066B/1790